Renegade

Steele Standing

Jacqueline M. Sinclair

Renegade

ISBN 978-0-692-57581-9

Cover photo: Andrei Vishnyakov

Cover design: Donna Osborn Clark of Creation By Donna

Editor: Wendi Temporado of Ready, Set, Edit

Formatted by: Donna Osborn Clark of Creation By Donna

Published by: Ink Fling Publishing

Printed in the United States of America

First Edition

To XXX
for giving the shy girl a place to grow.

Renegade

By
Jacqueline M. Sinclair

Table of Contents

Chapter 1 - William
Summer of 1969

I saw it as soon as my parents led me out the door and onto the front porch. A huge smile replaced my look of confusion.

"I'm proud of you, son."

My dad's words rang out from the steps below, and I eased past him and my mother, my attention focused on the brand new car parked on the street. I curled my fingers into fists and resisted the urge to pump them in the air. My father slapped me on the back in a silent 'You're welcome'.

"You need something of your own."

I heard the jangle of keys as he released them into the air, and I cupped my hands to catch them, a stupid grin still plastered on my face. I had something of my own, my mother's hand-me-down Chevy, but it didn't compare to this. This was *way* past need.

Trying to keep my cool, I walked to the street, running my finger along the raven-black paint on the hood as I walked to the driver's side door. I was nineteen. I'd just been given the keys to a brand new Shelby GT500. The town of Bradford would pay hell tonight.

"Be careful, son," my mom warned as I walked away. She didn't bother hiding the concern edging her voice. She had every right to be nervous. I'd been talking about owning a Shelby modified Mustang since they'd hit the streets, and I had full intentions of burying the speedometer the first chance I got.

"Have fun."

Climbing into the driver's seat, my grin widened with my dad's words. I wrapped my hands around the steering wheel, feeling the heat of the seat on my back and legs. The smell of new surrounded me, and suddenly I was unsure if I wanted to break her in at the county line or by getting Vicky in the backseat. I stuck the key in the ignition and fired her up.

I gave a last look to my parents, pulled the shifter down to drive, and stomped my foot on the gas. The engine's purr grew to a roar, and the tires spun from the burst of power. Half a block down, I jammed on the brakes and spun the wheel. The rear end slid around, fish-tailing, but straightened itself in the direction I wanted to go. Honking the horn as I passed back by my house, I didn't look at my parents. My mother would be horrified by my driving while my dad would be secretly shooting me two thumbs up.

Dialing in the radio, I found a station and sat back, cruising to the diner with my arm draped over the passenger seat and my thoughts on Vicky. Her folks had moved to Bradford and bought the diner to get away from the 'scandalous environment' that was Hollywood. She was hot, experienced, and had hit the town like a tornado—exactly the kind of girl to get my attention.

Shipped off to finish her senior year at a private girl's school before joining her parents, Vicky had arrived in full-on rebellion. We'd been fooling around ever since she got to town. Then, a week ago, she announced her parents' would be cutting off her support unless the rumors of her exploits stopped *right now*. Going steady seemed a temporary solution to keep my world spinning a little longer, so what the hell?

I had given some brief thought as to why her parents were at their wits end so quickly. I had a vague idea that the scandals they were leaving behind were a product of Vicky's making, but at the moment, Hollywood was a world away, and I couldn't give a shit less what her parents thought.

Pulling into the diner, I parked up front, blowing the horn in short bursts to clear a hole in the group of kids hanging out in the parking lot. Leaping out, I tossed my chin up to the Wednesday afternoon crowd closing in around me and the car. Hands shot out congratulating me on my new ride; hands tugged at my t-shirt as I passed through the group; girls begged for rides; guys asked to drive. But I was over it. My focus now was my girl, putting wheels on the pavement, and burying myself somewhere warm.

"Regina, where is she?" I yelled as I pushed through the glass door. The woman behind the counter rolled her eyes as she finished drying her hands, not bothering to look at me. She hitched her thumb over her shoulder toward the supply room without a word. I ignored her obvious irritation at my arrival and, never breaking stride, pushed through the swinging doors.

"Hey, babe…" The sentence stuck in my throat. Anthony Beckman jerked away from Vicky so quick she stumbled right back into his arms. "What the fuck?" I growled, my gaze pinning her to where she straightened herself, fumbling with the buttons on her pink and white uniform.

"Will—"

I cut her off. "Hell no. I'm not in for this high school bullshit. You're mine, or you're not." I stepped back, running both my hands through my hair. Vicky gave up on collecting herself and threw her arms in the air.

"Listen to me," she pleaded.

My heart was pounding in my ears. "A week, Vicky. We've been going steady for a fucking week and you do this to me? Me?" It was almost fucking comical.

I couldn't believe it. I had stayed single so I wouldn't have to cheat and now, my first official girl was cheating. Caught red-handed.

"What the hell," I groaned.

I could deal with her girlish flirting. I could deal with her lying to other people. I could deal with a lot, but I would not deal with another dude's hands on what had been given to me.

"Please listen to me, Will."

With composure that surprised me, Vicky finished buttoning her top as she talked and then smoothed her blonde hair. "You know you don't give a damn about me. We can talk about this."

She was right, but it didn't make me feel any better about what she was doing. "Talk? What the hell do we have to talk about?" I shook my head. What were my friends going to say about her stepping out on me? "You're lucky." I stopped, a rueful laugh escaping my lips. "No, *I'm* lucky to have found out now." I couldn't believe how low she'd sunk. "Making out with some jock in here with the pancake mix and ketchup?" I couldn't keep the surprise from my voice. I took her by the shoulders and backed her away from me. "It's a good thing for you I don't hit girls." I turned to Anthony. "As big a pussy as you are, that doesn't apply to you."

Before he could decide which way to duck, my fist met with his jaw and Anthony's head spun right, the momentum taking his body with him. He collapsed on top of an oversized trashcan, and both he and the container rolled to the floor. I walked calmly out of the storeroom with Vicky shrieking like a banshee, bobbing back and forth, unsure if she should help him or chase me.

Chapter 2 - Margaret

I DIDN'T LIKE BABYSITTING those children. Jacob Anderson's little boy was a terror on two legs, and that little girl of his must have been a princess in a former life. She was needy, spoiled, and tortured her poor brother until I was ready to pull my hair out.

Their father, in all of his misguided wisdom, was laying the world at their feet, and those poor little souls, they were stomping it into the ground. What I wanted to do was scream, take a switch, and give them all some good licks, Mr. Anderson included.

I felt bad that his wife had taken off, too. Who knew where she was, but society wasn't getting any favors from their father by giving in to their every foot-stomping tantrum. My parents would never have tolerated that behavior from me.

Barely a month into the summer, and I was already looking forward to the little buggers going back to school. At least then I could get back into my routine and away from them, except for after school. Drawing in a deep breath, I said a silent thank you that I'd made it through.

The only saving grace to this horrible day was the weather. It had rained yesterday and today—everything seemed fresh, new and bright. The trees that lined the street, purposely planted at regular intervals, were swaying gently in a soft breeze that made the heat tolerable. Traffic was light, the workers for the day having made it home to prepare to do it again tomorrow. The only thing that disrupted the peaceful walk home was the occasional squeal of children playing while they waited for supper to come off the stove.

Approaching an intersection, I was vaguely aware of a car coming from my right. They'd have a stop sign. I looked behind me to make sure I wasn't walking in front of anyone turning and stepped into the street. The squealing of tires was instantaneous. My body turned toward the sound and froze as the black blur bore down on me, smoke rising from the beast as it skidded across the asphalt toward me.

I froze. There was a fire in my chest. I forced the heat out of my lungs and inhaled sharply, desperate to ease the burn. My numb body was shaking. My eyes burned. The smoke — the breeze had blown the acrid smoke right into my face. I blinked. My knees gave way, and I hoped my bladder hadn't followed.

The man who'd been driving the car was by my side while I was processing the fact that I was still alive.

"Are you all right? Jesus Christ, answer me, are you OK?"

I wavered, caught only by the arms that wrapped around me and supported me as I stumbled to the safety of the curb. He was speaking to me, but all I could hear was muttering mixed with the pounding in my ears and a curse word spat here and there. He left me long enough to pull his car from the road and then came back. He waited, fidgeting until my panicked breathing eased, my body recovering from its near-death experience. Then he lit into me.

"What the hell were you doing in the road?"

My body stiffened. Fear and anger collided, but I couldn't manage to put the storm of thoughts racing through my head into coherent words.

"There…stop sign…you…didn't…" I reached in my purse and pulled out a tissue, ashamed that I had fallen apart. I dabbed the tears from my eyes before they streaked down my face. He was the one who ran the stop sign.

"Damn." He pulled his legs up and rested his forearms on his knees. He locked his hands together and bowed his head.

"Fucking shit," he groaned. "I'm sorry. I wasn't paying attention. Fuck. Can I at least take you home?"

His apology brought my anger to the surface. No, I didn't want this maniac to take me home. I found my voice. And my wits. I reached out, blindly shoving him out of my space. "You almost killed me. Are you insane?"

My shaky attempt to push him away barely caused him to teeter on the curb. He turned to me, pulling my face to him with a gentle tug. My eyes fell closed, a feeble attempt to keep him from seeing the tears that threatened to spill at any moment.

"Are you OK?"

I started to nod that I was, but the rough feel of his palm against my cheek became like a wave of warm water splashing through my body from the inside. I forced my eyes open. My blood drained to my feet, taking my heart with it. I knew who he was. Of course he was insane; the whole family was.

My expression must have said it all. The corners of his lips tugged as if he was trying not to smile. I knew who he was, and he knew it, but he introduced himself anyway. "I'm William. William Steele. Or, just Will."

Deep dimples hugged the expression on his lips before his cocky grin faded into uncertainty. I refused to be in awe of him. I gritted my teeth and forced a smile. "Well, thank you for not running me over, William Steele."

I pulled my head from his hand and stuffed the tissue back into my purse.

"How far do you live?" he asked, ignoring my sarcasm.

I'd lived in Bradford my whole life. I didn't need to look around, but I did, taking in my surroundings while I tried to collect my thoughts and stall for composure. My heart was racing again, and it had nothing to do with his driving.

"About four more blocks. I'll be fine, really. Thank you." I was all talk. My hand was shaking against the concrete curb even as I tried to push myself to my feet. He stood and offered his hand.

I eyed him. The last thing I wanted was him aware of the trembling I was having.

Ignoring his hand, I sat my purse aside and used both hands to push myself up. Not trusting my legs, I took a moment to straighten my skirt and take a deep breath before I tried to reach down and collect it. William beat me to it.

"Thank you," I stammered as he held it out to me.

Reaching for my purse as I stepped away, William refused to let it go. "What's your name?" he asked.

I swallowed the pool of saliva I was producing. "Margaret."

Turning toward home again, William released my purse and fell into step beside me.

"You don't have to walk me home."

"I'm not walking you home. I'm walking you to the park."

I stopped short. "I don't think so, William." I'd heard the rumors. I knew what kind of man he was, the things girls had done with him, and how they whined and cried when William never called again. Did he think I was that kind of girl? My cheeks burned at the thought.

As if reading my mind, William grinned. "Talking won't corrupt you, Margaret, and neither will I, unless you want me to, anyway." He crossed his arms over his chest, and all I could focus on was the spot where his white t-shirt strained against his skin. For a moment, I wondered if there'd be a cigarette packed folded in the other sleeve. I dared a peek before I raised my gaze to his eyes. He was watching me, amused.

"Or, do I scare you?" he asked.

Looking up to him, my body dwarfed by his, I studied the subtle flakes of gold that swam in his brown eyes. It was such a unique and beautiful combination that was only emphasized by his tanned face. William obviously enjoyed being outside. He waited patiently while I finished my assessment with his right eyebrow slightly cocked and that smug twitch still playing on his lips.

"No, William, you don't scare me." The lie was so quiet I wasn't sure he heard me until he swept out his hand in a chivalrous wave and invited me to walk with him. The knot in my stomach snatched tighter. When we were on our way, William glanced over at me. "Do you have a last name, Margaret?"

"Wilson. Margaret Wilson."

Our hands bumped as we walked, and I made a point of putting a little more distance between us.

"Why don't I know you, Margaret Wilson?"

Cutting my eyes at him, I couldn't bite back the laugh. "You're not exactly in my Sunday school class."

He seemed to consider it for a moment, ignoring my dig. "Surely I've seen you around."

I shrugged at his comment. "I'm sure you weren't looking."

He grunted. "I don't know how I missed you."

"Five minutes ago, I think we were both glad you missed me," I said, ruefully.

William was nodding. "I was distracted. I'm sorry."

It was on the tip of my tongue to ask what had been distracting him, but William changed the subject.

"Will this get you into trouble?" he asked.

"What?" There were so many things wrong with this picture I couldn't pinpoint just one "get me in trouble" decision I'd made in the last few minutes. My mother would be worried if I was late coming home and didn't call. My dad would be upset because I'd left my mother longer than planned, and to do what? Hang out at the park with the worst bad boy in town?

I decided to turn the tables and avoid the question altogether. "Wouldn't it be *me* who gets *you* into trouble? The whole town knows you're with Victoria."

"No, I broke up with Vicky. Why do you call people by their full name?"

"Because it's their name." I didn't have to think about it. "I wouldn't want someone calling me Marge." I crinkled my nose at the nickname even as I spoke it.

William shook his head. "You're definitely not a Marge."

"When?"

"When what?"

"When did you break up with her?" Moments ago I would have been mortified to be asking such personal questions of a man — any man, but especially one with a reputation like his. The fact that Victoria was going steady with him — or had been — had been pouted over by practically every girl in town. She'd become the girl everyone loved to hate, but put up with in hopes they could see a little more of William.

Now, as we strolled down the sidewalk with the sun behind us and our shadows stretching out before us, I felt entitled. Maybe because he'd almost killed me.

With a straight face, William looked at his wrist. There was no watch there. "About twenty minutes ago."

We came to an intersection. Straight would take me home, to the right, the park William mentioned.

"Crossroads," he pointed out, eyeing me. "I know you're not scared of me. That got us this far, Margaret." He added an accent to my name so that it rolled off his tongue as *Marguerite*. "Now, do you trust me?"

I may have grinned at the fancy nickname, but no, I didn't trust him. But I was drawn to him. All the fine hair on my body was on end, and my anxiety was balanced by curiosity. I hesitated to answer.

"Tell me no, and I'll walk you home. We'll keep to the main road so there'll be plenty of talk and gossip, but no real threat." He leaned into me as if his next words were a secret. "Tell me yes and we go to the park." He straightened and smiled and my resistance began to melt. "There's still no real threat," he said. "But only the possibility of rumor and gossip. Which will it be?"

Chapter 3 - William

ONE WEEK OF EXPECTING Vicky, that whore, to be loyal had been too much to ask. Truth be told, I was more embarrassed that my friends would find out she'd stepped out on me than I was hurt. My attitude shifted into *I don't give a damn* mode looking at Margaret, her staring back at me as I rambled off her choices.

"I guess we'll have to see about that."

She was smiling, and that was enough for me. My ego was thriving again. Pride washed over some of the embarrassment I was feeling about Vicky. Grasping her hand in mine, I turned us toward the park. I'd never been one for this affectionate bullshit, but this one was hard to read. Despite the steel backbone she had when she'd given me shit for almost running over her, I wasn't sure she wouldn't change her mind any moment and skitter away.

"Back at the car you looked at me like you knew me, or at least know who I am. Does that bother you?"

"We're talking. What's it going to hurt?"

Her words were stronger than the look she offered with them, and I tilted my head in her direction, silently calling her on her explanation.

She gave a small shrug. "How are you any different than all the other boys around here with a fast car and freedom?"

Money. Reputation. There were half a dozen reasons why this town singled me out. When I didn't argue, Margaret continued.

"You graduated third in your class, so school wasn't something you turned your nose up at. It was obviously important to you. You didn't quit, and you did well." She took a breath, looking toward the sky as if she was calling to mind all the things she'd heard. "What you have is the unfortunate circumstance of being preceded by your family that, though generally law-abiding and successful, has a history of pushing those boundaries."

It felt like she was repeating years of gossip. "That's a mouthful. Is all that rote garbage your way of telling me you've heard *some* good things about me?" I asked.

"Yes."

For the first time, a genuine smile lit her face. I was enjoying myself more and more. "You are direct, Marguerite. How do you know my class standing?"

Approaching suppertime, the park was practically deserted, so I led her to the empty swings. I held the chains while she settled into the seat and gave her a gentle push.

"Victoria has been pointing out what a great catch you are…were…since you two started going out. She's all about your good deeds."

I stifled a grunt at the mention of Vicky. "Why do you think she did that?"

"I'm sure she had her reasons."

There was only one I could think of — she was half-excited being with me and half-ashamed. My family had made their money running moonshine during prohibition and had multiplied it by turning to legal manufacturing when the Volstead Act was rescinded. My family no longer ran on the back side of the law, but the money was tainted. We were outlaws then and according to the town, we still were. My grandfather and his father's generation were still regarded as legends, and it was only the money and jobs that Steele, Inc. brought into the town that held us in society's good graces. My limited virtues placated her parent's feelings about Vicky's walk on the wild side.

"Truth be told, Marguerite, I did it all for the car."

Her easy laugh echoed in the air around us. "I'm not surprised. I'd do almost anything for a car like that, too." She composed herself. "You want to tell me what happened?"

Her question stirred me. Her tone was genuine — concerned — and I found myself entrusting my shame to her. I gave her another gentle push before sitting in the swing beside her.

"I went to the diner and found her wrapped around Anthony Beckman."

Her feet went to the ground, stopping the swing. "You can't be serious."

For a moment, I frowned at the surprise in her voice, but I could feel the muscles in my face relax as the humor of it all washed over me. Anthony had excelled in school and frankly seemed to be a little outside of Vicky's general realm of reach. I, for one, had found my extracurricular activities outside of school and word that I had been cheated on, with the likes of Anthony Beckman, a jock, would give the town something new to talk about.

"What did you do?"

"What any self-respecting man would do. I hit him."

Margaret's hand flew to her mouth. She turned in her seat to look at me. Her face was impassive, and I couldn't help but wonder if disgust was hiding behind those beautiful green eyes. Would she want to leave now?

"He had to know you were with her," she finally said.

I nodded again, confirming he did. "Amazing what men will stick their dick into."

She blanched at my words, but her thoughts seemed to be stuck on the fact that I'd hit him. "Do you feel better for doing it?"

"No," I admitted. "I feel better having met you." The confession rolled off my tongue before I had the good sense to stop it. Our eyes met and the moment was over. She stood.

"I need to get home. My mother will be wondering where I am."

Sucking up my disappointment, I fell into step beside her. We walked in silence a bit while I turned over the burning question. "Could I take you to dinner sometime?"

She snorted, and I cringed at the sound, trying to tamp down the wave of anger growing inside me.

"I don't think so, William. I'm not what you're looking for."

For the second time today I was being blown off, and it didn't sit well with me. It was not something I was used to, yet a little devil was whispering in my ear, *that's who you are, asshole*. I didn't like it, and my irritation poured out in my words. "What exactly do you think I'm looking for?"

Her hand landed on my arm. "I didn't mean it like that. It's just, well, my folks are strict, William. I can only go out on Saturdays. I can have friends over during the week until eight, but I volunteer at the hospital Tuesday and Thursday evenings. I can't have company at all on Sundays. That's our family day." She withdrew her hand and crossed her arms over her chest but kept walking.

The way her voice faded with disappointment made me regret this line of conversation, yet, I couldn't stop the argument from spewing out of my mouth. "How old are you?"

"I'm eighteen, but it doesn't mean I don't have rules."

Her tone reeked with insult, but still, I pushed. "It's summer. You still can't go out except Saturdays?"

She considered it. "I haven't had a reason to ask."

Her words settled between us, and I understood; little Marguerite didn't get out much. "OK. Well then, let's plan on Saturday. I'd like to take you to dinner. Or something."

"I don't do, *or something*. I repeat, again, wrong girl."

There was a hint of exasperation in her voice. This chick was fire and mischief wrapped up in sweet and shy, and my interest went up a notch. This girl was way outside Vicky's league, and my charm wasn't even touching her.

Margaret had come to a stop in front of a white, picketed gate and was looking at me with something I took as dismissal. Time was up, and I had yet to get a yes from her.

"So, no dinner?"

She ignored my invitation, letting herself into the gate and closing it behind her. She waited with her hands resting on the wood, looking at me with an expression of intense sincerity.

"I think Anthony got what he deserved. Victoria will, too."

Her statement did little to soften the blow. She was rejecting me, telling me no without saying it. One last, gorgeous smile and, with a toss of her curly red hair, she disappeared inside.

Chapter 4 – Margaret

WILLIAM'S OFFER HAD BEEN tempting, but I had made it through high school with my head down, managing to stay out of gossip and away from the attention of the mischievous kind of boys; I didn't want to start now. Life was cruel enough in this cardboard box of a town, and I didn't want rumors of what I did…or didn't do…upsetting my parents, especially now when they had enough going on.

I wasn't lying when I told William my parents were strict. Mom had been less so since she became sick, but my dad, despite the extra shifts and the pressure of Mom's illness weighing on him, was as vigilant as ever. The fact that he was working so many extra shifts merely meant that he relied on a verbal update from me regarding my habits. He had no reason to think I would lie to him, and I was so disciplined it hadn't occurred to me until now I had the freedom to do it.

William Steele didn't fit into my life any more than I fit into his. Walking away was the best thing to do, but I could feel him watching me. I could feel unasked questions pulling me back to him demanding answers. Shutting the front door behind me was a challenge, but I did it, leaning against it to listen to the sound of quiet that greeted me.

Mom must be resting. I went to the kitchen to start dinner. Tonight would be spaghetti, and I was making enough for my dad to take to lunch tomorrow and still have enough left for supper tomorrow night. It was Wednesday and already felt like a long week with those Anderson children. I wasn't looking forward to another night of cooking after being at the hospital. Leftovers it would be.

Browning the hamburger in a pan, I put water on for the noodles. My thoughts drifted back to William, and for an instant, I regretted telling him no. Well, ignoring his question. I never did get around to telling him no, but I got the feeling he would argue my point, and I would lose. I knew I would. He was outside my norm. He was exciting and dangerous, and he didn't just push boundaries, he plowed through them. In the safety of my house, out from under those searching brown eyes, my mind couldn't help but consider what it would be like to escape the safety of this house. For just a little while, I would like to forget about the growing problems and the neat little package my life was meant to be and escape with him, if only for a night.

With everything on the stove, I picked up the phone and dialed Tammy's number. My best friend answered on the second ring, out of breath, but with a whimsical, "Hello."

I knew she was happy. Ecstatic; she was leaving for college at the end of the summer and putting this town behind her. I bit back my jealousy.

"You're in a good mood."

"Yes, I am." I could picture her, her lanky frame bouncing on her feet as she held the phone, and suddenly I regretted calling. I no longer wanted to tell her about William. I didn't want to hear the lecture she would give about him being no good for me or the trouble he would bring. I was smart enough to figure that out by myself. I decided to keep it to myself and let my secret simmer.

"Why? What's going on?" Even I could hear the obligatory sound in my voice, and I felt worse that I couldn't be happier for her.

A brief silence had passed between us before she answered me. "I'm going to Granny's the week after next. Mark is going to drive us down that Tuesday."

I was a little surprised. Mark was three years younger than Tammy; he hadn't had his license long, and the fact that their parents were letting the two of them take off on a road trip was shocking. Mine would never consider such a thing.

"That should be fun." My voice managed to find some enthusiasm, but it was a struggle. I realized Tammy had detoured the conversation because she knew I was upset about having to put off college. That's just how she was, but it made me feel worse.

"It will be. It also means that I need some time with you before I go. Let's hit the diner Saturday. My treat. I need to see you before I leave."

I stretched the cord to reach the stove and stirred the hamburger while we talked.

"Better yet, see if you can stay over."

The thought of an all-nighter with Tammy made me smile. It may be the last one we'd have before life got in the way.

"Sounds good. Are you coming back before you leave for school? Maybe we can do it again before you go."

"I'll be back a little less than a month. We can do it again. It'll have to be a spur of the moment thing, though, because I've got shopping and stuff to do, other family to see."

"Spur of the moment will work." I really wanted to remind her that I had no life, and whenever would be fine. I rolled my eyes at my growing self-pity. "I'll see you Saturday."

We said our goodbyes and hung up. I was looking forward to it. I finished supper and went to find my mom. She was in her room reading on the bed. She smiled at me, and the muscles in my stomach tightened. At least today she looked like she felt good. She patted the bed beside her, and I sat down as gently as I could.

"How were the kids?"

"Terrible."

She giggled, knowing they were terrors. "Did you talk to Mr. Anderson about them?"

I shook my head. I had one time, but not since. He hadn't taken my meddling very well, and I've been sensitive about bringing it up again.

"He's stressed, sweetheart."

"I know," I said. "But it isn't helping them."

She nodded her head in understanding.

"Supper is done. I talked to Tammy while I was cooking. She wants me to have a sleepover Saturday. Is that OK?"

"Of course it is. You girls are going to miss each other."

Mom was right. Tammy and I had been accepted to schools on opposite ends of the country, only she was still going to college, and I wasn't.

"She's leaving early to visit her grandmother. She'll be back before she takes off for good."

Mom sat her book face down on the bed to save her page. "Well, you go on and have a good time. Your father and I could use a night to ourselves, too." She climbed off the bed. "I think I'm going to have a bath before I eat. I'll clean the kitchen when I'm done." She leaned across the bed and kissed my cheek. "Thank you for cooking, Margaret."

I watched as she closed the door to their bathroom and drew a deep breath, tears stinging my eyes. Today was a good day, and I was grateful for that. I pushed myself up and went to my room to change. If I could just make it two more days, I'd have a whole twenty-four hours with Tammy and escape reality for a bit.

Going to my room, I decided I wasn't very hungry and flung myself on the bed. Once again my thoughts drifted back to William Steele. Why would he, of all the boys in this town, ask me out on a date? *Not a boy, he's a man. All man.* And trouble.

Rolling onto my side, I pictured his face, his cocky smile, and how it faded into disbelief when I didn't jump at the chance to be his date. What did I have to offer someone like him? The wave of free love spreading across the country hadn't washed over me, but the thought of William touching me — kissing me — created a need I wasn't used to and even then, heat flittered through my veins.

I sat up too quickly. He wasn't supposed to stir those types of feelings inside me. With a groan, I collected my pajamas and went for a bath of my own.

Chapter 5 - William

THE SATURDAY CROWD AT the diner was small, but it was early, so I parked on the back side, walked around to the group hanging out at the picnic tables, and found myself a seat. Vincent Bradford took a seat beside me, slapping me on the back as he straddled the bench.

"Where ya been, asshole?"

"Hey, man. I've been around." I was distracted, trying to listen to two other guys talk about a race in the chaos of all the other conversations. Adrenaline was already seeping into my system. They were meeting up in a neighboring town, and that was all the better; the competition here had started pulling out when I pulled up.

"I hear you're single now. That didn't last long."

That got my attention. Vince was my buddy, but my business was my business, and I was ready to put a quick stop to his mouth. I turned, seeing he was leaning in for privacy. He wasn't being a dick about it, and my irritation tamped down a bit.

"Yeah. She's a fucking whore, man."

"So I hear." Vince took a last drag from his cigarette and flicked it out into the parking lot. "The whole fucking town has heard about it."

I flipped my palms up, dismissing his words. What could I do? For a day or two rumors were rampant about Vicky and what she'd done. After that, I was crucified about the things I had to have done to push her to it.

Vince mumbled something about California cunts and lit another smoke. Nodding to the growing crowd discussing the race he asked, "You headed to the heat?"

"Thinking 'bout it." I could already feel the rush. "You going?"

Vince frowned. "Naw, man. My clutch is gone. I had to hoof it up here."

I turned around, leaned back, and propped my elbows on the table. "You going to fix it?" Vince's Nova had seen better days, but he'd been fixing and hopping up the engine since he bought it. The body was shit, but the engine was a masterpiece. He'd fix it.

"Soon as I get the dough."

"Let me know, I'll help."

Vince grinned. "You got the time with this 8-5 bullshit you're doing now?"

"I'll make time. You're not the only one with connections."

Vince let out a long whistle about the dig. He wasn't offended. His father was a douche, a political douche who remained an idol in the town because his family had founded it. Vince was a pimple on his ass—a very painful, embarrassing pimple—but like most towns, the people ate up the crap that was fed to them.

"I can help."

Vince went into a list of other things he wanted to do if he could ever finance his dreams. I let him rattle on, my attention caught by the red-head striding toward a tall, dark-haired girl waiting by the front doors of the diner. They hugged and started talking. I backhanded Vince's chest, nodding their way.

"What do you know about that one?"

"Which one? The short one is a dead fish. Hang that up, asshole. But that other one, she's got a wild side."

"Man, shut up." I wouldn't exactly describe Margaret Wilson as a dead fish. Maybe a little cold, but she'd been warming up to me. I cocked my head toward him, watching the girls as they disappeared inside. "You game?"

Vince's eyes widened, and a smile grew on his face. "Hey, man, it's speed or need. I'm up for either."

"We're out," I announced, pushing myself up. I walked away, and Vince fell in beside me.

"You know that chick?" he asked.

"No, but I'm going to."

I heard him chuckle as I pulled open the glass door and stepped in. "Good luck, man."

Scanning the booths for Margaret and her friend, I knew I was going to need it. We walked over and slid in beside them, me beside Margaret and Vince with her friend. Conversation came to a standstill as the two girls eyed one another and then us.

"What are you doing?"

Margaret's tone was hushed but heard by everyone at the table.

"I asked you to dinner."

Her friend sucked air and looked at Margaret, her mouth hanging open.

"I didn't say yes, William."

"You didn't say no, either." I reached across the table, offering my hand to Margaret's friend. "William Steele, nice to meet you."

"Tammy Whitfield." She closed her mouth and shook my hand. I nodded to Vincent. "This is Vince."

Tammy nodded. "We've met."

She gave Vince a look, and I knew they'd done more than meet. Bastard was holding out on me. "Have you ladies ordered yet?" I looked at Tammy, who still seemed to be sorting all this out.

"William, you can't do this," Margaret hissed.

Across the table, Vince slid closer to Tammy, resting his arms on the back of the bench, prepared to enjoy the show. Tammy had gotten some color back in her cheeks, but she was still eyeing Margaret like she was a three-eyed monkey.

"We all have to eat," Vince told her, grinning.

On cue, the waitress walked up, and Margaret was too polite to make a scene in front of her.

"What are you getting?" Margaret's cheeks were flaming red when I turned to ask her, but she spilled her order to the waitress. Tammy rattled hers off next. Vince fell in, and I went last.

"Same ticket?"

The waitress wasn't very friendly, but what did I expect? I gave her my best fake smile. "Same ticket." She rolled her eyes at my sarcasm and walked away.

"She likes you." Tammy had finally recovered and was grinning.

"It's my charm." Everyone laughed but Margaret, who seemed to slink down into the booth. Her body jerked, and Tammy gave her a tight smile. I turned away trying to hide the grin. I was pretty sure Margaret had just got the equivalent of a swift kick in the ass under the table.

"What are you guys doing tonight?" Tammy asked.

Vince turned his body in her direction. "What do you want to do?"

Tammy raised an eyebrow as if she was open for the challenge. I snuck a peek at Margaret, who looked like she wanted to reach across the table and punch her friend in the face.

"This is supposed to be us."

Tammy turned her full attention to Margaret. "I'm not ditching you."

The waitress returned with our drinks, sitting them on the table without a word and took off again. I reached under the table for Margaret's hand. She pulled away, wrapping both hands around the sweating glass of soda. I settled into the booth. I can be patient. I don't like it. I don't do it often. But for her, for now, I would be.

Tammy and Vince kept the conversation going, and the friendly banter seemed to help Margaret relax. I put my hand on her knee, squeezing a little, but not going any farther. Margaret's hand went under the table taking mine in hers. It may have been an attempt to keep it from creeping up any further, but I took it. I wrapped my fingers around hers and stroked the back of her hand with my thumb. She didn't pull away until our food came, and when she did, she brought my hand up with hers.

Vince prodded, still trying to find out what they were up to. "What are you ladies doing tonight?"

Chapter 6 - Margaret

"MARGARET IS SLEEPING OVER at my house."

I could feel myself grow heated just from the perverted look Vincent passed to William.

"We wanted one last sleepover before Tammy leaves." Christ. That didn't help. Vincent's eyes went wide with amusement, but William waved him off before anything could leech from his mouth.

"Where are you going?"

Thank God for William for redirecting the train wreck that was about to happen. I was a little more at ease since we'd begun eating, and William was forced to move his hand away from my thigh. Even with the cotton of my dress between us, I could still feel the heat from his touch, and the warmth seemed to spread further up my body the longer his hand remained.

"Visiting family and then I come back for a month and then off to college."

"Cool. What are you going to study?"

"Law."

Vincent coughed. Not just a reflexive, trying to be funny cough—he was turning red, and Tammy reached out, pounding him on the back.

"It's not that bad."

Vincent shook his head, still coughing. "Fucking shit." He barely managed to squeeze out the words while the rest of us tried to act like it wasn't happening. Grabbing his soda, he gulped it down, draining the glass. He slammed it on the table, taking a few deep breaths and glaring at each of us. It was our undoing. The entire table erupted with laughter. Vincent wiped the tears that had formed in his eyes. The red glow slowly faded from his face as his breathing returned to normal. He chuckled, finally caving to the fun and laughed along with us. That was it. We had bonded.

"You people just going to sit there laughing and let me die."

"Hey, I patted your back," Tammy argued.

Vince shook his head and popped a fry into Tammy's mouth. "Eat your food, and let's go for a ride."

Vincent looked to William, the only one of us who had a car. He gave a nod, and I went from admiring Tammy and Vincent's easy connection to almost having a panic attack. I couldn't leave with them. *We* shouldn't leave with them. My heart was pounding in my ears. I had always envied Tammy's adventurous side, right up until that moment. Beads of sweat were gathering in places I didn't think could sweat.

I wasn't very hungry all of a sudden. The thought of trying to swallow food past the lump in my throat made me nauseous. What had I gotten myself into? I'd barely managed five words to William since he'd sat down. It hadn't been like this at the park. I felt cornered, and I lashed out.

"Have you lost your mind? We are not going."

Vincent didn't miss a beat. "Want her all to yourself?"

The raging blush was instant. Lucky for me, Tammy was pushing him from the booth, and it was lost on them both. "Let's go. Come on, I'm done."

My shame was not missed on William. Blocking my exit from the booth, he was watching me, his lips cocked in an almost entertained grin. With his eyes on me, he eased from his seat so I could climb out. He gave a bow. "Marguerite."

I eyed him with more contempt than I felt, but still he raised an amused brow at me as I brushed past him and headed for the door. I tried not to think about the people who I was sure watched the scene unfold until I was standing in the parking lot, hands on my hips asking William where he'd parked.

He didn't answer. Instead, he smirked and pointed his finger toward the back of the parking lot. At least the spectators wouldn't see me leaving with him. I climbed in the passenger seat and shut the door, forcing Vincent and Tammy to climb into the backseat from the driver's side.

"Done with your tantrum?"

The question came from Vincent and was followed by the smack of skin on skin and a yelp from him. William looked at me. He wasn't amused. He wasn't angry. He was grinning, victory written all over his face.

Pulling his door shut, he started the car. Christ, I had been acting like those brats that got on my nerves all week. I rolled my eyes and threw my hands up in defeat. William's grin grew to a full-blown smile, and I felt like my heart flipped in my chest at the sight.

Tammy pushed my shoulder from behind, reassuring me. "We have plenty of time."

We could go hang out and still make curfew. Her parents insisted on one. No self-respecting lady was out after eleven o'clock, and she would be a self-respecting lady as long as she lived under their roof. The problem with Tammy was there was nothing that could be done after eleven that couldn't be done before. So here we were, speeding through town headed to who knows where and no one knew.

"Turn it up." Tammy grabbed the seats, pulling herself into the front, bringing me back to the conversation. She reached for the radio and managed to find just enough friction on the dial to turn it up. The sound of The Foundations filled the car. William tapped his finger on the steering wheel to the opening beat and started singing along as soon as the words to "Build Me Up, Buttercup" came through the speakers. I was in awe. He exuded happiness at that moment. I was smiling. Tammy joined in from the back, quickly followed by Vincent, and I was all at once swept up in the mischief, liberated from worry.

I joined in on the next chorus, matching William's moves as he danced in his seat. He threw his head back and laughed. I was lost. His brown eyes were shining, crinkled with laughter. The dimples melted into deep parentheses that hugged his lips and hid the mask of recklessness William was known for. My heart captured the image and tucked it away. *This. This is William Steele.*

Chapter 7 - William

THE ONLY PLACE I knew to head was the lake. I pulled onto the two-lane road that would dead-end at the water, hoping it was early enough that no one else had already claimed it for the night.

I slowed the car as I topped the hill. Thankfully, the road was deserted. I eyed Margaret as I pulled a few yards from the water's edge. She was looking out over the water, the glow of the sinking sun shining on her face. Damn, she was beautiful. Not in an instant hard on kind of way, but there was something about her that reached beyond her green eyes and red hair. Something that seeped from her that demanded attention in an, *I can't look away*, kind of way. How had I never noticed her?

Leaving the windows down and the radio on, I climbed out and sat on the hood of the car, my back against the windshield. Margaret followed but hesitated. "You sure you want to lie on your car? Isn't it new?"

I patted the hood. Tiny little Margaret wasn't going to hurt my car if I wasn't. "Come on. The sun will be gone in a few minutes."

She looked toward the lake like I might be lying, but she climbed on, putting her hands under her legs. *I'm such an ass.* The engine was hot, and her thin dress wasn't going to do much to protect her. I slid off the hood and walked around to her side. I held out my hand. "Let's watch it from the water."

Margaret took my hand before I even finished. I led her toward the small beach, waiting as she stopped at the asphalt's edge and pulled off her shoes. I did the same and with her hand back in mine, we walked to the water, following the waterline until we were out of sight of the car. I pulled Margaret into my arms, locking my hands behind her back. "I'm glad you came."

With her face looking out toward the water, the gentle breeze blowing her hair around her face, I couldn't see her expression, but I felt the tension in her body. I got the feeling she was in unfamiliar territory. She wasn't angry, but the happy-go-lucky Margaret I'd gotten a glimpse of in the car had disappeared. I planted a kiss on the top of her head. "Let's go sit."

I found a log and propped against it, pulling her down into my lap. I circled my arms around her waist again and waited. A few times she sucked a breath like she was getting ready to say something, but she didn't, and I didn't press her. Mostly because I was afraid of what she'd say.

With a final, ragged breath, she leaned her head against my chest, and we watched the last explosion of light streak across the sky as the sun sank behind the trees. Not a word was said, and I was OK with that. Margaret had relaxed in my arms, the distant sound of the radio becoming clearer as the night unfolded. Nothing more was needed.

I kissed the top of her head again, and she snuggled into me. Even *I* felt the chill coming off the water, but neither of us made a move to head for the shelter of the car. Vince and Tammy were there and at the moment, I was unwilling to share Margaret with anyone.

I ran my hand down her arm and took her hand in mine, splaying her fingers and running my fingertip over her nail. "Are you glad you came?"

"You guys didn't give me much choice," she said with a grunt.

"You don't sound mad about it."

"I'd be lying if I said I was. This is nice."

She shivered.

"Except for the cool wind blowing off the water?"

I let go of her fingers and ran my hands up and down her arms, slowly but deliberately generating a warming friction. I looked out over the water at the broken reflection of moonlight dancing on the waves. I was struck that not once since I'd been with her had I thought of the racing I'd missed. More shocking, now that I had thought of it, I still didn't regret not going.

"You think it'll be cold up there?"

Margaret nodded toward the moon. NASA had just launched astronauts into space, and the whole world was raving about the US putting a man on the moon.

"I'm more concerned about them being able to breathe when they get there."

"You think there's going to be trouble?"

I shrugged against her. "Hard to say. We've never been to the moon before."

Margaret adjusted in my arms. "Would you go?"

"You're dreaming. No. I don't think I'll ever leave Bradford, and if I did, it wouldn't be to go to the fucking moon."

Her head rolled against my chest. I was sure it was in response to my language. "How'd you find this place?"

I folded her into my arms to try and keep her warm. "My grandfather use to bring me fishing here."

I dipped my face into her neck, feeling the heat radiating off her skin. I breathed out, letting the moist air warm my face. Margaret shivered again, and I pressed my lips against her moistened skin. Her sharp intake of breath forced me to do it again.

"William."

Her voice was gruff and laced with confusion.

"I can't. I'm not ready for this."

I buried my teeth into the sensitive skin of her neck. Her shoulders and hips pressed into me as her body arched against the feel. Her fingers dug into the outside of my thighs. The effect on me was immediate. I released the suction and grazed my lips across the spot before doing it again.

Tightening my arms around her, I pulled her into me so she could appreciate my reaction. Margaret pressed her face to mine as if to push me away, but it only intensified the moment. She was panting in my ear, and the escape of each warm breath brought a fresh wave of need over me.

"William, don't."

A rush of air pushed passed my lips. I wouldn't. I couldn't. I pressed my lips to her ear. "I won't." I held her close, collecting myself. I didn't usually have this problem. With any other girl I'd been hanging out with, we'd have been rolling in the dirt an hour ago. This wasn't what I wanted with her.

We returned to our comfortable silence until the clouds rolled in and hid the moon.

"If we're going to be on time, we have to get going."

Making curfew wasn't something I'd bothered with in a long time, and taking her home wasn't something I wanted to do. Still, I stood with mixed emotions. What made this girl so different?

We were all grown, yet I was struck with a feeling of being responsible for something as ridiculous as getting the girls home by curfew. "See, you're safe."

Margaret's huff told me she disagreed. My mind was racing, and each recall of her subtle reactions snapped another cord of my self-control.

Margaret brushed off her dress, despite that she'd been sitting in my lap. I dusted the sand from me and took her hand in mind. "Does this mean I can take you to dinner now?"

"You did tonight."

Rolling my eyes in her direction, I pulled up short. "That is *not* what I mean." I turned her toward me, taking a moment to take in the gentle expression on her face. She was tired, but a hint of humor came through and quickly faded.

"This isn't a good idea."

I didn't like where this was going. "For who?"

Margaret looked away. I cupped her face with my hands and brought her gaze back to me. "I won't make you regret it."

She was thinking about it. My insides clenched with impatience as she sought reassurance in my eyes.

"OK."

"Saturday?"

"Saturday," she said.

I tried not to grin like a fool the short distance we had to the car. The windshield was steamed up, and I pounded on the hood, giving Vince and Tammy fair warning we were there. Margaret looked away as if the two could be seen putting themselves back together in the backseat. It was cute, and I thought, *this is why I can't push her, why we weren't down at the water still, rolling around in the dirt.* She's different. And for once, I wanted — I *needed* that. More than anything.

The passenger side door opened, and Tammy crawled out, straightening her clothes. Vince fell out behind her, stretching and shaking his head. He wasn't happy about the interruption.

"You ready to go?" Tammy was talking to Margaret, who looked at me.

"We should."

She didn't say she was ready, at least. The night had served its purpose. I had my date with Margaret, and for the first time in a long time, my life felt balanced.

Chapter 8 - Margaret

WILLIAM DROPPED US OFF at the diner with a smug smile. "I'll see you Saturday."

I shut the door to his car and walked away, a thousand thoughts racing through my mind. *Would he show up? Would he expect to pick up where we left off tonight?*

Tammy and I walked to her house. She didn't say much, and I wasn't sure if she was just distracted by her night with Vincent or if she was angry with me for being a stick in the mud. "You OK?"

She pulled her lips to the right and bit her bottom lip. It was her method of concentrating. "I'm confused, Margaret."

"You like him, don't you?" I was smiling, trying to find the motivation to tease her like a best friend is expected to, but I just didn't have it in me. The look on her face warned me she wasn't in the mood. My thoughts were bouncing between being in William's arms at the lake and the anticipation of our date on Saturday. I snapped my mouth shut and finished the walk in silence.

Her father greeted us at the door, giving Tammy a welcoming hug and a goodnight kiss all at once. Upstairs, we changed into our pajamas. Tammy sat on the side of the bed.

"What's wrong?" I sat down beside her, pulling my mass of curls into a ponytail to prevent a tangled mess in the morning. She didn't answer.

"What's wrong?" I asked again, but Tammy just stared out into nothing for a moment.

"I'm not sure what happened tonight," she finally said.

"What do you mean?"

Tammy sighed. "He's a gearhead; not much drive for anything else. No ambition. But, I like him. I like him a lot. How can I do this?"

For a girl that had been pushed her whole life to succeed, Tammy had always seemed to take the pressure well. She was decisive, strong-willed. She had her goals, had since I could remember, and with the exception of a wild hair once in a while, nothing deterred her. Seeing her waiver in a decision made me uncomfortable.

"Maybe cars *are* his ambition, Tammy."

She seemed to consider it, so I pushed the issue. Hadn't I just agreed to a date with William Steele? Ambition may not be his problem, but his reputation was. I was qualified. "Nothing wrong with cars, is there?"

"He wants to see me when I come back from Grandma's."

"Nothing wrong with that."

"I'm leaving for school, Margaret. How can I get involved with him when it's time to leave? What am I supposed to do, leave my heart behind?"

Tammy stood, tugging the covers down. I moved out of her way, and she climbed into bed without another word. I didn't know what else to say. There was nothing else *to* say. Climbing onto my side of the bed, I pulled the covers to my chin and closed my eyes, replaying bits and pieces of the night, my mind constantly recalling the image of William laughing and singing in the car. Regardless of how moody he may seem, that is the image of him I would always remember.

The week was more of the same. I silently prayed every day before walking into the Anderson home that I could survive without beating one of those children, or Mr. Anderson. By the time I left in the evenings, I was drained. Exhausted. But, I had a mentally prepared list of everything my children would *not* be when the time came.

I didn't hear anything from Tammy. I hadn't really expected to. She was still withdrawn when she'd gotten up Sunday morning, so I quietly collected my things, gave her a hug and left.

"I'll call you when I get back."

That had been enough to tell me I wouldn't see her again before she left, but I missed her already.

Walking home from the Anderson's on Friday, I was mindlessly staring into store windows as I made my way down the sidewalk. A display caught my attention, and I studied it through the pane. I couldn't remember the last time I'd bought a new dress, or been willing to part with the money to buy much of anything for myself. It seemed like as good a time as any.

Pushing inside the store, I went to the back side of the display and studied the emerald green dress. The black buttons were a nice contrast and the flared skirt was a little…sassy. With my mind made up, I went to find a saleslady.

"Excuse me. I'm interested in the dress in the window."

The tag pinned to her blouse read Judy. She looked me over, presumably assessing my size and smiled like a woman who'd just made a sale. "I'll be right back. You can try it on in there."

Judy pointed to a closed door in the far corner of the store as she walked away. I browsed around, waiting for her to return when the bell over the door chimed with the arrival of another customer. Victoria.

I smiled politely, but she breezed by me toward the back of the store where the more personal items were kept. The fresh face she'd worn when she'd arrived in town was gone. She seemed stressed, and I turned, watching her disappear among the shelves.

Judy reappeared, the hanger in one hand and the skirt of the dress draped over the other. "This is going to look just beautiful on you." She tilted her head toward the back of the store. "Come with me, and let's see if I picked the right size."

Judy hung the dress on the back of the door and came out so I could go in. The tiny room was barely big enough for one person, but the mirrors on each of the walls gave the appearance of space. There wasn't. My elbows banged into the mirrors more than once, but I finally got the dress on. I huffed, taking a moment to recover from the wrestling match I had just had before taking a look at myself in the mirrors.

"Hurry the hell up. Let's go."

The gruff voice was followed by stumbling and a muffled thud, as if someone had caught themselves from falling.

"I just need…"

"Go."

The booming voice cut Victoria off mid-sentence. I glanced at the mirrors to make sure I was covered where I needed to be and pulled the door open. By then Victoria and Anthony were making their way to the front of the store, and it was over.

I shook my head, surprised at this obnoxious version of Anthony I saw for the first time. "Some tiff," I muttered, shutting the door, again.

A closer inspection did nothing to change my mind. I was in love with the dress, the color — it was going home with me. I slid it off and put it back on the hanger. It would be perfect for my date with William on Saturday. I dressed again and headed to the register, finally glancing at the price tag. I tried not to show my shock at the $8 it would cost me.

I was nervous about William meeting my parents, and I briefly wondered if I should warn them or avoid it altogether. They weren't exactly judgmental people, but they hadn't yet had to deal with their sheltered daughter running off on a date with a boy — a man — let alone one whose reputation was known throughout the county as trouble. I wavered back and forth until destiny solved the issue by providing much-needed overtime for my dad at the plant. He wouldn't be home, and I was granted a reprieve.

The hours dragged by on Saturday. I spent the morning doing chores, the little things my mother normally took care of. Dusting, vacuuming. I cleaned out the refrigerator and pulled the freshly dried towels off the line and put them away. I took a last look around the house, searching for something I missed, anything else that would fill my time. Nothing stood out. The linoleum was sparkling from the extra energy I'd had last night. The countertops were spotless, and everything that had a place in the cabinets was there, out of sight.

I moved to the living room, my feet sinking into the thick, recently vacuumed carpet. Flecks of disturbed dust floated in the rays of light that spilled through the open, pale-blue curtains, but the oak end tables and the coffee table were clean and free of clutter. The pillows of the brown living room furniture were perfectly fluffed and in place. Nothing else to be done here.

Upstairs, I went to my room and looked through my closet for the tenth time, making sure nothing else had appeared that I'd rather wear more than the perfect green dress I'd spent way too much money on. There wasn't, and I hit the shower with the chorus of "Build Me up, Buttercup" replaying over and over in my mind.

I was getting nervous. Who was I kidding? I had been nervous since I'd met him, and my anxiety was only winding tighter the closer six o clock came. Trying to relax under the warm spray of water, I washed and moved on to my hair. By the time I turned the water off and stepped out, I had wasted so much time, I felt like it was running out.

I dried off and pulled on the dress. My hair, a genetic gift from my mother, took extra time. Taming the wild curls was a constantly changing art form that varied day-to-day depending on the weather. Except for lipstick, I didn't wear makeup so, fifteen minutes before William was due to pick me up, I was ready and pacing the floor.

Did he think it strange that I'd never been on a date before? I'd hung out with friends at the diner. I'd gone to the movies with my girlfriends, but that was rare because our town didn't have a theater. I hung out with boys at church functions and talked to them on the phone. But, I'd never been picked up at my house and taken for a real, honest to God date. I was nervous. Would he even come? A week had gone by, and we hadn't even talked. Maybe he and Victoria had worked things out. She and Anthony hadn't seemed all that happy.

My mind created a thousand excuses that my heart tossed aside. Why couldn't someone like William Steele be interested in a girl like me? I sought my reflection for an answer that eluded me. I turned from the mirror and went downstairs, turning out the light as I left the bathroom.

If I could find something to do in the kitchen, maybe I could fight the butterflies in my stomach. My mom had made a rare appearance, having moved from her bedroom to the comfortable and recently-fluffed couch and was curled beneath a blanket. She was pale, and water seeped from her eyes. Guilt washed over me.

"Mom, I can stay if you're feeling bad."

She adjusted herself and reached out to me, taking my hand. "Your dad is only working half of that extra shift; he'll be home soon. I'm fine."

I squeezed onto the couch beside her, wiping a wisp of hair from her face. There were moments she was more confused than others, but it seemed time had all but come to a standstill for her.

Sometimes she didn't seem aware that I should have been preparing to leave for college or that I had put off going to school, that it was a poor time for me to leave them and that we were, in fact, too poor at this point for me to go.

"Tell me about your date."

I was so much like her it was like looking in a mirror sometimes. Except, I had the healthy glow of youth while Mom's skin was tinged with yellow and swelled over her skeleton like the padding of a costume. Her eyes hadn't glowed with anything but pain since before we found out she was sick. Dad was constantly working to help pay the doctors, but he was never too tired that he slacked in his dedication to her. He never complained about how needy she could be on bad days, and I admired him for that. Today she was weak, and her voice was tired and raspy. I forced myself to focus on the conversation.

"I met him on the way home Wednesday. He graduated last year and works with his family."

"Yeah? What do they do?" Her eyes drifted closed, edging more seepage from the corners. I dabbed at it, delaying.

That was the part I wasn't looking forward to, and a small part of me hoped she wouldn't remember or recall the name. "They own Steele, Inc." I felt my body tense even as I said the words.

Her eyes fluttered open in surprise, and I tried not to cringe, waiting under her scrutiny.

"He's obviously made an impression on you. I won't judge." A smile played on her lips even as her eyes drifted shut again. My anxiety dropped a notch. At least I wouldn't have to endure the whole meeting of the parents. I refreshed her glass of lemonade, put it back on the coffee table and resumed my pacing.

At 6:05 I checked the driveway to make sure William wasn't sitting out there, waiting. At 6:30 I began fighting back tears. He'd said he wouldn't make me regret it. At seven, I went to bed and let them come.

Chapter 9 - William

MARGARET'S DAD ANSWERED THE door wearing pinstriped pajamas, his thinning hair sitting like dried grass on his head.

"I need to see Margaret."

He looked me over and pushed the door a little tighter. "Do you have any idea what time it is, son?"

I hadn't bothered to check the time. I'd hauled ass over here as soon as Vince passed out. I stood a little straighter. "I'm sorry, I know it's late. I need her."

Mr. Wilson was shaking his head before I even finished. "That's not how this house operates. You need to leave."

He went to shut the door in my face when Margaret appeared at the top of the stairs. "What are you doing here, William?"

I stuck my foot in the gap, keeping him from closing it. *Margaret.* Her quiet tone was just loud enough to reach me. She leaned her hip against the banister, crossed her arms, and waited. Tears welled in her puffy eyes and spilled quietly down her tear-stained face. My heart slammed on the brakes. What had I done? I put my palms on the door and pushed, forcing Mr. Wilson to step back far enough to let me in. He would not keep me from her.

Taking a step forward, I entered the house. Mr. Wilson, apparently not knowing or caring what was good for him, moved to block me from the stairs, and I found myself standing face to face, almost nose to nose, with Margaret's father. Looking past him to Margaret, I clenched my fists, angry at myself, angry at him for standing in my way, at this whole fucking situation.

"I need your help." There was no reason for her to trust me. I'd let her down. The disappointment was all over her face, and I wouldn't blame Mr. Wilson if he jacked me up against the wall at this moment.

Her hand went to her hip. "To do what?"

"I'll explain in the car. Please, Margaret."

"She is not leaving this house. You need to go. This is the last time I'll tell you this."

I ignored him, silently begging Margaret. I was running out of time. "I'll explain everything if you just come on."

Margaret cut her eyes to her father, considering her options. His back was to her, but he must have sensed trouble in her hesitation. Mr. Wilson turned, stomping toward the kitchen. "You won't be going anywhere with my daughter."

Fuck. He's going to call the cops. I didn't need that right then. There was too much to explain. I looked at her father's retreating back and then gave her one more pleading look. Nothing. She was frozen in place. "I'm sorry," I groaned the apology and turned back toward the door. I had to go. I would just have to fix things with her later.

Margaret's bedroom shoes slapped against the wood as she descended the stairs and ran out the door behind me. She was crawling into the passenger seat by the time I pulled open the driver's side door.

"Where are we going?"

Margaret was looking at me, taking in my appearance, and I knew she was assuming the worse. "The hotel."

"William, what's happened?"

Her voice was laced with anger. Fear. The unknown. "Vince is hurt."

"What do you mean, hurt? What am I supposed to do?"

"You work at the hospital, Margaret, he needs help."

"William I don't work at the hospital. I'm a candy striper. You can't be serious. What's wrong with him? What am I supposed to do for him?"

The totality of the situation slammed into me. Vince was in bad shape. Margaret had just walked out on her father to come with me. This wasn't going to get any better. I pulled the car down a side street, taking the back way to Bradford's only hotel. I hoped like hell she could do something, but I needed to warn her.

"He's pretty beat up, Margaret."

"You guys were fighting? William, if you're going to get me into more trouble than I already am, just take me home."

I shook my head. "I'm not going to get you into trouble, Margaret. He's not in good shape. I don't know what to do for him."

"Who were you two fighting with?"

"We weren't fighting anyone." For fuck's sake. I doubted that Margaret had ever encountered anything like this, and I didn't know how to explain it, to warn her. We were pulling into the hotel, so I ignored her question. Instead, I emphasized what I'd already told her. "You won't get in trouble for helping."

She gave me a, *we'll just see about that*, look and climbed out of the car. I came around, taking her hand and led her to the door. I slid my key in the lock and eased the door open. Vince was lying on the bed where I'd left him. I stepped out of the way and pulled Margaret into the room.

"Christ." The ragged word drifted from her lips, and I turned to see her taking it all in, inching back toward the door. "William is he…"

I stepped to her, pulling her hands into mine, but she was still studying Vince. "He's just passed out."

"He's drunk?" Her eyes scanned the room, taking in the empty cans littering the floor and table by his side of the bed. "William, he needs a doctor."

"He wouldn't go. They'll know him and call his dad."

"His dad needs to know." Her voice was tight and high with panic.

"Oh trust me, his dad knows all about this."

She spun toward me, her green eyes bright with emotion. "His dad did this to him?"

I swallowed hard, wishing I'd been a little gentler in breaking this to her. "He has before. Not this bad, but yeah."

Her eyes widened in disbelief, but she pulled from my hands and moved to the bed.

"Vincent?" She put her hand on his shoulder but didn't attempt to shake him. Vince didn't move. Margaret folded some of the covers back to get a better look at his face. I saw her tense, her lips drawing back in a grimace.

I was having a hard time balancing the anger inside me with the voice of calmness I felt Margaret needed to hear. "I think his dad jumped him to get the upper hand and then proceeded to just beat the shit out of him," I said.

"We need to get him turned over and undressed. There's probably more than we can see. I need towels and warm water."

I headed to the bathroom at the back of the room.

"But, William?" I stopped and turned back toward her. "We find anything we can't handle, and he goes to the hospital. I'm not going to keep him here if we can't help him."

I gave a nod and went to gather everything she asked for. I filled the ice bucket with warm water, grabbed all the washcloths off the rack and took them to Margaret. "Help me get him on his back."

Margaret had the covers pushed to the floor, and I eased Vince from his side to his back while Margaret pulled his shoes off.

"Help me get his shirt off."

Ripping the thin t-shirt up the seams, I pulled the rest over his head as gently as I could. Not much could be seen on his stomach. There was a red mark around the lower part of his neck where it looked like his shirt might have been snatched from behind. A bruise was growing over the left side of his ribs. Margaret gently pushed her fingers against the area.

"I don't feel any of them moving, William, but I'm not a doctor. I don't think they're broken."

I kept my mouth shut and let Margaret continue to look him over. The knuckles on both his hands were scraped, with more bruises on his arms like he'd tried to defend himself. Some minor scrapes along his elbows and forearms were probably from the concrete floor of the garage.

"Roll him over for me."

Margaret walked around to the opposite side of the bed and turned on the bedside lamp. I rolled Vince to me and held him on his side so she could see his back. Margaret's eyes flew to me, and I leaned over the bed to see what she'd found. A long, red, arrow-straight welt ran down his back from just under his shoulder, midway down his back. Bruises were growing from the entire length of the mark, and there was a matching wound midway down his back that disappeared into the waist of his jeans.

"What would do this?" she asked, looking at me. Unshed tears sparkled in her eyes, and I felt the burden of having brought this ugly into her life.

I shook my head. "A pipe? A tire iron maybe?"

A single tear spilled over and eased down her cheek. She brushed it away and tugged at his jeans.

"They need to come off, too. I'm going to get some soap and towels. We need to get his face cleaned up and check his head."

Chapter 10 – Margaret

I TURNED ON THE water and leaned over the sink, fighting back nausea. How could a man do this to his son? Squeezing my eyes shut to prevent a flood of tears from running down my face, I took a few deep breaths to regain myself. Could I do this? What if Vincent was worse than he looked, and I missed something?

My stomach was in knots. We should carry him to the hospital, even if we had to go to the next town. A dozen consequences ran through my mind, but I couldn't grab hold of any single one to stop this disaster. Vincent was grown. But, how far would his dad go? What would happen if the hospital called him, and what kind of trouble would he make if they did? The man was a pillar of the community. Bradford was practically built by his family. Was he capable of this? I thought of the cuts on Vincent's hands. He'd fought back. Or had he started it? No, William said his dad had been doing this his whole life. So why had no one stood up for Vincent before it got this bad? My mind didn't have the experience or ability to process this. I ground my palms into my eyes.

What have I gotten in to? I said a silent prayer for strength and turned off the water. I grabbed the tiny bar of soap and ripped the paper from it and pulled the few towels from the rack. It didn't really matter how I'd gotten here—I was, and Vincent needed help. What else mattered?

I went back to the room. William had Vincent's pants off as well as the sheet that was covering him. He saw me coming and pulled it down far enough for me to see that the line stopped halfway across Vincent's right butt cheek.

"OK, roll him to his back so we can get his face cleaned up."

William eased him down, and I went back around to the other side of the bed. Vincent's face was a bloody mess. His nose was swollen, but it didn't look broken. It was hard to tell with all the swelling, but it wouldn't kill him. Both eyes were bruised up, and there was a deep gash oozing blood on his left cheek.

"Probably wasn't a good idea to get him drunk," I grumbled.

I dipped a washcloth in the warm water and rung it out, dabbing at the bits of crusted blood before adding some pressure to try and stem the free-flowing stream. "This should have stitches. We're going to need some ice. The cold might help stop the bleeding."

Without a word, William left the room and returned a few minutes later with another bucket overflowing with ice. He got a fresh washcloth and filled it with ice.

"Can you go around and hold it to his face while I check his head?"

"He wanted a few drinks. I thought it would help calm him down, and I could change his mind."

"Change his mind about what?"

"Going to the hospital."

I ran my fingers through Vincent's hair trying to feel for any cuts that might be hidden. "How long has it been since you found him?"

"I was going to pick him up and drop him off at the diner on my way to get you and I found him like this."

It was all William offered by way of explanation. I pulled my hands away, checking my fingers for fresh blood. There wasn't any, and I didn't feel any bumps. This would be so much easier if Vincent was awake and could talk.

"Keep that on his cheek."

Taking the bucket to the bathroom, I emptied it and refilled it with warm water, returning to clean his hands. With the towels folded under them, I opened the cuts and let water drip from the washcloth to rinse out the deeper ones. Not only were they bloody, but there was grease from where he'd been working on his car embedded in the cuts. *Maybe it's a good thing he's not awake.*

"He's going to be hurting tomorrow."

"I'll go to the store as soon as it opens and get him something for pain."

I cleaned the cuts as best I could. "There's nothing else I can do for him, William, but watch him. He still could have hit his head, have a concussion or something. I'd feel a lot better about this if he was up and talking."

Nothing about this situation made me comfortable. I took the buckets to the bathroom and dumped them down the sink, and went back and checked the gash William had been holding pressure on.

"He was talking when we got here."

I ignored William and gently probed Vincent's cheek. The seeping had stopped. "It's probably going to open back up. That's a bad cut, and it'll be a bad scar."

William rolled off the bed and took the ice bag to the sink, dropped it in, and washed his hands. I cut the far lamp off and came back around, gathering the folded, wet towels and pulled the covers back over him. I gave him one last look. Despite the bruising, his color looked good. He didn't seem pale. His breathing was nice and deep. I closed my eyes and ran through the situations I'd been exposed to, steps doctors had taken, treatment nurses had provided. My head hurt from the effort. *What if I missed something?*

I felt William's arms wrap around me, and he hugged me to him. "Thank you." He kissed the back of my hair, and I leaned into him from pure exhaustion.

Leaning past me, William turned off the remaining bedside lamp so that the room glowed with just the light that filtered through the perimeter of the curtains. He swept me up in his arms and carried me to the overstuffed armchair that sat in the corner of the room. Easing into the chair, he draped my legs over one arm and cuddled me against him.

"Get some sleep."

Thirty seconds ago that would have been an easy thing to do. Now, the top to my pajamas had ridden up and was tucked under William's arm. It had pulled the front just high enough for William's fingers to find skin, and his thumb was tracing gentle lines across my ribs. I wiggled in an effort to provide more coverage, but it only served to give William more available skin to caress.

"I'm sorry I hurt you, Margaret." His hushed words were followed by the gentle kissing of my hair just above my ear, where his lips lingered a few moments. "I swear I'll make it up to you."

I snuggled farther into his lap. "I thought you'd blown me off." The admission brought the horrible thoughts back with such vividness that my body tensed. I had imagined William had found someone more fun, someone that didn't have to rush off to get home or was more willing to speed things up when I had been constantly slowing him down. William's arm tightened around me, and his hand squeezed my flesh into his grip.

"I saw it on your face the minute you came down the stairs."

"I felt like such a fool."

William's hand slid up the skin of my back and folded me into his chest. "I came for you as soon as I could."

Risking a glance in the dim light, William kissed my forehead, my nose. "What are your parent's going to say about you running out tonight?"

Blowing out a long breath I shook my head and leaned back against him. My father would be livid. Ashamed. How would I explain this to him? Would my mother understand? I couldn't think about that right now. My brain was still trying to reconcile Vincent's situation with what I knew a father to be. I couldn't come to terms with it. There was no way I was going to sleep. I needed to get home, but I was leery of leaving Vincent, afraid to face my parents. I was torn and exhausted. And then there was William. I squirmed in his arms. I didn't want to leave him just yet.

We sat in silence, William with his cheek resting on my head. I was comfortable but emotionally restless and William knew it.

"I feel like such a dick for standing you up. I think I needed to see you as much as I needed your help. I didn't know what to do."

I stifled a yawn, despite my chaotic thoughts. "I can't imagine you being scared of anything."

William groaned. "I have my moments. When I was little, I climbed a tree in our backyard and was too afraid to come down." He kept his voice low as if he would disturb Vincent. "It was just inside the wood line where I could still see the house. I couldn't have been more than four or five years old. I got my ass up in this giant oak tree and sat, looking at the back of our house, thinking how cool it was. Then it started getting dark, and I looked around and all of a sudden it seemed so high I was scared to move."

William's fingers had traveled down my back and were now splayed across my stomach. "What did you do?"

"It felt like I sat there for hours. I was afraid to yell for my dad. I knew he'd be mad. I knew my mom would be looking for me, and she'd be upset when I didn't come home. I also knew that would make Dad even madder."

I giggled at how William's young brain must have processed all this while his fingers swept circles around my stomach, starting small and widening with each pass. "It got so dark I started hearing things in the woods. Sticks were breaking. Animals were moving. There was howling echoing through the trees. I was crying like a little girl by then."

The first time his fingers brushed the swell of my breast I froze, holding my breath and waiting. I should have gotten up, demanded to go home, but I didn't. He stopped with the circles and started tracing my cleavage with a single finger. His finger traveled up my throat and fluttered across my collar bone before sliding slowly down my shoulder, my ribs and back to my side before making another slow pass. His low whisper was hypnotizing, and his soft touch was taming my anxiety. I was staying.

"By the time I decided whatever was in the woods was worse than what was in the house, I figured out how to get out of that tree. I don't remember my mother ever hugging me so hard."

He sighed at the memory, but I was distracted by the fingers gliding down my ribs. I couldn't move. I could barely recoup the soft breath that escaped me. My mind was screaming at me to get up, to stop this before it went too far. But, the devil had me in his hands and with excruciating skill he was molding me into someone I didn't recognize.

I swallowed hard. William's touch never ceased. His lips were at my ear, his cheek against mine. "Relax. We're not going to have sex right here with Vince in the room."

My face burned with embarrassment. "I barely know you," I breathed.

"But, you want to know me. I bet your panties are already wet." The touch of amusement in his voice quickly faded into a low growl.

How could he know? "Are you goading me, William?" My tone was no longer mindful of Vincent sleeping—passed out across the room. "You haven't even kissed me, and you have your hand up my shirt."

"Are you saying you don't like it?"

His voice in my ear was as sensual as his touch, and my traitorous body shivered at the truth in his words.

A low moan of approval rose in his throat. "Your body doesn't lie."

Chapter 11 - William

SHE WHIMPERED IN MY arms, and I felt myself harden even more. This was about the dumbest damn thing I'd done. What I wanted to do was drag her to the bathroom and bend her over the sink. Even if he had been awake, Vince wouldn't care, and at the moment, I didn't think she would, either. Her rhythmic breathing and soft sighs were like a song I didn't want to end. So I kept on playing the game. A fool's game.

"Would you prefer my tongue?" Goose-pimples flared on her skin. I moved the arm that was cradling her and fisted my hand in her hair, tilting her face to me.

"William."

The lusty sound of her voice went through me, and my eyes fell shut, letting the sound echo in my mind. *This woman.* Christ. I hadn't even *kissed* her. What was the hold-up?

I leaned in until I felt the warmth of her breath on my face. Would I be able to stop with a kiss? Touching her was torture, and this was a fucking mistake. It couldn't be like this. Not with her. Not tonight.

"Go to sleep, Marguerite." I moved to kiss her forehead and laid her head against my chest. I pulled my hand from the front of her shirt and wrapped it around her waist so that she was locked in my arms.

It took some time, but I knew the moment she went to sleep. Her body relaxed and her breathing eased and became steady. Resting my head on the back of the chair, I tried to pull my thoughts together. It had to be getting close to 4 AM. I would need to call my dad. I considered having Margaret call Tammy in the morning; I was pretty sure Vince had been sneaking around, seeing her, but, it was way too early for all that right now. Besides, he'd be pissed enough to know Margaret was here and knew his dad had been beating his ass for years.

Instead, I settled in and watched until the blinking neon light filtering through the window was washed out by the morning sun. I laid Margaret on the bed beside Vince and pulled some of the covers around her. He hadn't moved. He'd probably be out a little longer, so I grabbed my keys and drove down to the store on the corner, trying not to grin at the image of him waking up to find her next to him.

At the store, I grabbed Band-Aids, peroxide, and everything else I could think of. I went to the phone booth and dialed my father's number. He answered on the first ring, wide awake.

"William?"

"Hey, Dad, yeah, it's me."

"Where are you? You're lucky your mother isn't out looking for you herself."

My dad couldn't give a damn less if I came home or not, but a courtesy phone call was expected. I could imagine my mom was having a conniption. I gave him a quick rundown on Vince's situation, rushing through the details.

"And how long has this been going on, son?"

"For as long as I can remember."

The confession brought an extended silence. "Not like this," I explained. He was disappointed I hadn't helped my friend before it had gotten to this point. Vince himself shrugged off the bruises, admitting to provoking more than his share. I had failed him. I had been too busy running the roads to put my nose in Vince's personal business and help my friend escape his own father. It would not happen again.

"He's sleeping. Doesn't look like it's anything major, but he beat the fuck out of him."

There was a moment of silence on the line. "One of these days that man's going to get what's coming to him. I wish you'd have told me about all this sooner, William."

I should have. Vince's father might could do no wrong in the eyes of Bradford, but my father was a Steele, and he would stand with me. Even with Vince complaining, "Who's going to believe me? I'm a flunky," my father would have done *something*.

Deep down, I was sure there was some shame, too. A guy as big as Vince getting pushed around by a drunk, especially one that showed a whole different face to the town, wasn't something anyone would be proud of. Sucking in a breath, I said, "I should be getting back before he wakes up."

"You take care of Vince today. Don't worry about work, but call us if you need us."

"I will. I don't know what he's going to do yet, but I'll stay in touch. Thanks, Dad."

I hung up, stretching out the stiffness from sitting in the chair for hours. Going back into the store, I picked up some snacks and drinks and headed back to the hotel. Easing the door open, I found Vince and Margaret sleeping much like I'd left them.

Cleaning up the cans Vince had downed, I straightened the room and took my seat back in the chair. I considered bringing Margaret back into my lap, but there was such a peaceful look on her face that I couldn't bring myself to disturb her. Instead, I watched. I thought, and I shook my head.

What the hell had I been thinking, dragging Margaret out of her house in the middle of the night? Her parents would never let me live this down. Margaret may never see me again after facing her parents over this. The girl had probably never done anything to get punished in her life. Hell, even Tammy sheltered her, to an extent.

Vince rolled over with a groan, pulling me from my misery. He lay there a minute before raising his head, looking around the room. He saw me before his gaze landed on the sleeping figure beside him. He pointed to her with a questioning look.

"Margaret," I said, quietly.

His left eye was swollen shut, but his right eye shot up. "What the hell?" Vince didn't do tact very well, and his voice carried his surprise. Margaret flinched beside him.

"Shhh." I stood, going to his side of the bed. "How are you feeling?"

"Like I've been beat the fuck up. And you're going to put me in a bed with a cold fish? Like this?"

"Relax, man, she wasn't here for fun. Besides, she's not like that. She does some work down at the hospital. She checked you out."

Vince was moving slow, but raised the covers and peeked beneath. "I see she did. Where are my clothes, man?"

I nodded to a corner of the room.

"I bet she was proud of that," he muttered.

"She just came to help. It's good. I'll go to the house and get you a shirt later. Need some aspirin?"

"A whole goddamn bottle if you got it."

I searched the bags and found it. I grabbed him a Coke and brought it back to the bed. Vince rolled to his side and pushed himself up, biting his lip to control the grunt of pain rumbling in his throat. "Fucking Christ."

He took the aspirin and dumped four in his hand, washing them down with a long swig of soda before setting it on the bedside table. I leaned against the wall, crossing my arms.

"What do you want to do?"

He grunted. "I want to take that fucking baseball bat to his fucking head."

I shook my head. "Dude, I think it was a tire iron this time. He's going to kill you one day if you don't do something."

Vince shifted, bracing his hand on the bed to take some weight off his back. "I got to get the fuck out of here, Will. This town…I can't stay here."

Crouching, I rested on my haunches with my back against the wall. "Tell me what you want to do."

Chapter 12 - Margaret

I LAY THERE IN silence, listening to William and Vincent plot his escape. My heart was breaking for him. How on earth could life be so terrible that a child had to run from his father? I couldn't imagine, but like Vincent said, what was in Bradford for him?

"Right now I'm going to run a scalding bath and put my sore ass in it."

Vincent's weight lifted from the bed with a groan, and I closed my eyes until I heard the bathroom door shut.

"You can get up now, Margaret."

My eyes flew open. How had he known? The bed dipped beside me, and William's arm wrapped around my waist. "I spent half the night listening to you sleep; I knew you were awake."

Heat flamed my face. "It never seemed to be a good time to say anything."

"It's a mess, isn't it?"

I could only nod, feeling unshed tears burn my eyes. It was so unfair. I couldn't believe it, yet, here we were.

"Ready for me to take you home?"

No. But, I couldn't stay in the hotel room with William forever. My parents would be irate regardless of when I came home, but there was no need to drag it out.

"Cops might be looking for us."

That didn't make me feel any better. I let go of a shaky breath. I didn't think my father would call the police on William if

I were with him, but I also didn't think fathers beat their children with a piece of iron.

"Are you going to stay with Vincent?"

William had nestled his face into the back of my head, and I felt him nod.

"How long are you going to stay here, at the hotel?"

"Until we figure out how to get his car and get it fixed."

"How are you going to get it? He just said his clutch was out."

"It's doable. Not good for the car and kind of tricky, but it can be done. He'll be up to it in a couple of days."

"Will he stay here until then?"

William blew out a long breath. "I hope so. He can go to my house, but when his dad sobers up, that's where he'll look."

I didn't like William's explanation, but it made sense. The nerves that had been in my belly since I'd walked into this room tightened. I rolled over, coming face to face with him. "I guess I should go."

His brown eyes staring down at me searched my face. "You OK?"

This time, I nodded, not trusting my voice.

"You did good last night."

I forced a smile and William's lips landed on my forehead. "Let's get you home before you're grounded for life."

William pulled the Shelby to the curb and cut the engine. "Want me to come in with you?"

Yes. My parents would be furious. But this was something I would have to deal with alone. Besides, I didn't need William to have another scene with my father. "I'll be OK."

"Margaret, I'm sorry again. For letting you down, for dragging you into this."

I waved off his apology. It seemed so long ago already. "I understand. I'm glad you could be there for Vincent. He needed you more than I did."

William offered a faint smile. He was tired, and it was beginning to show in his eyes. "You need me?"

I rolled my eyes, but I couldn't stop the laugh. "I'll see you later."

Without waiting for a response, I climbed out of the car, shutting the door behind me. I gave one last wave to William and went to face the fury of my father.

He was sitting in the arm chair in the living room when I walked in; his hands were steepled under his chin. I leaned against the doorframe, suddenly feeling the exhaustion of the night and the lack of sleep.

"You want to tell me what's going on?"

I thought about it a minute. "No, not really." It was Vincent's business and bringing my father into it didn't seem the right thing to do. His hands dropped to the arms of the chair, his face straining to contain his surprise at my defiance.

"I'll not have you traipsing off in the middle of the night with every hooligan in town. What is wrong with you, Margaret?"

"Every hooligan, Daddy? Is that what you think of me?"

He pushed himself from his chair. "Do you have any idea the name you're going to make for yourself? I'll not have this; I'm telling you right now."

Stepping closer to my father, I felt myself wilting from the stress. I don't know where the strength came from. "I'll not have you treating me like I'm some whore, Daddy. I am grown. You raised me. Have some faith in me." I couldn't hold back the tears anymore. They poured out, doing nothing to ease the ache of the last twenty-four hours.

"Your mother should not have to be dealing with you running off like this, Margaret. I didn't tell her this time. Are you really going to break her heart, acting like this when she's —"

I couldn't listen to anymore. Escaping up the stairs, rage was pounding in my chest. How dare he use my mother to make his point about William? Running to my room, I slammed the door and threw myself on my bed. I wished I had stayed at the hotel. I wished I could go collapse into my mother's arms and ask her why life did these things to people. Would she understand? The thought of disappointing her and adding to her burdens unleashed a fresh wave of tears, and I gave in to the grief.

Chapter 13 - William

THE LAST THING I expected to see at the door was Margaret. She looked worn, tired and her eyes were just as swollen as they'd been when I left her. My heart clenched. I had done this to her, brought this pain to her and I hated myself for it.

"How is he?"

"I'm alive," Vince answered her from inside the room. "You going to stand out there all night or come in like decent people?"

I stepped aside and let Margaret in, not bothering to warn Vince that Tammy was with her. He saw her, freezing with his soda at his lips.

"You couldn't call me, asshole?" Tammy, hands on her hips, stood at the foot of the bed looking like she was ready to take Vince for round two.

The can of soda floated down as Vince considered his situation. "Hasn't really been time."

He wouldn't have called her, period. I cut my eyes to Margaret, who was looking a little smug with herself. "I think we're going to go for a walk and let you two battle this out."

Margaret eased out the door of the room, and I followed, pulling it shut behind me. We walked out into the fading sun and fell in step, with no particular place to go.

"I think he's pissed you called Tammy."

Margaret shrugged with indifference. "No, he's embarrassed, but she cares about him. He seems better."

"He stayed in the bathtub for a while. He's still sore as all hell. I went and got him some real food. He's eaten. How about you? How'd things go when you got home?"

Margaret gave a nervous laugh. "Not very good."

I was sorry but glad she was back. "You surprised me. I wasn't expecting to see you again today."

"I wasn't expecting to come back. I hope it's OK. I took a nap, talked to Tammy and then she showed up. There was no stopping her. Did you know her and Vincent have been sneaking around for months?"

Taking her hand in mine, I tugged her toward the school. "I got some ideas about them the day at the diner."

Margaret cut her eyes to me, and I shrugged.

"She was raging because I didn't call her last night. I guess I should have."

"I wasn't sure how tight they were. Vince would have been even madder to wake up and find her there. Not that I think you'd care."

She shot me a quick smile as we entered a breezeway that would empty at a set of stairs to the second floor. Halfway through, I stopped, turning Margaret to me. "You know something?"

"What?"

I took a step that brought me face to face with her. "I think I want that kiss now."

She took a step back. "I didn't realize we were negotiating."

"If I remember last night correctly, you were willing then, Marguerite. Aren't you now?"

She backed away again, and I stalked forward until she was pinned against the brick wall of the breezeway. I planted my palms against each side of her head.

"I should have stopped you."

"Well, you didn't. Now, how about that kiss?"

Margaret swallowed hard. "If you'll stop looking at me like you want to devour me."

I would have laughed if her shaky words hadn't brushed across me like the stroke of her hand. "Make no mistake, Marguerite, I absolutely do want to. And I will."

Leaning down, I buried my face in her neck, planting a light kiss against where her pulse was pounding against her skin. I traced a short line with the tip of my tongue before gently biting into her neck. She gasped at the sensation, but tilted her head, opening to me, and I did it again and again. I leaned my body into hers so that I could feel her chest rise and fall with each pant that spilled from her. "How about that kiss?"

The subtle turn of her face toward mine was all the green light I needed. I caught her cheek in my palm. A soft brush of my lips against hers and I pulled away. Her eyes fluttered open, and she focused on me, drawing me back to her.

That time, my tongue slipped past her lips and met hers. Her arms went around my neck, pulling me to her, and I was lost. Margaret surrounded me. Her taste, her smell, the way she rested her body into mine. *This. This is what my life needs to be.* I pushed myself from her with my hand still held against the wall, taking a last breath of what was her — the moment. "Christ, Margaret."

She ran her tongue across her bottom lip as if she were savoring the kiss, the taste of me — us.

"We really should go." All but groaning, I grabbed her hand and led her back in the direction we'd come, my plans of sitting on the stairs and talking abandoned. Whatever Vince and Tammy were doing they better be done by now.

She was silent as we walked back, lost in her own thoughts. At the hotel, I knocked on the door and waited a moment before letting us in. Vince wasn't in a place to be doing much of anything, but you never know. He was lying on the bed where we'd left him with Tammy snuggled up to his chest. She looked from Margaret to me and back to her friend.

"Everything good?"

Tammy's question was directed at Margaret, but I answered. "Everything's good," I said. She didn't look entirely convinced, but she didn't push it.

I pulled Margaret to the end of the bed and sat down, bringing her with me. There was a brief silence, all of us trying to fight the awkwardness in the room. Vince ran his hand through his messy blond hair and looked at me. "I need to get my car, man, get it fixed. Think your folks would mind if I put it in their garage?"

William shook his head. "They'll be cool with that. When do you want to get it?"

"The sooner, the better, but it'll have to be when I can change those gears without crying like a bitch. My back and ribs are throbbing."

"Vince is going out west with me," Tammy offered. She was looking at Margaret, and I got the feeling it was akin to a private discussion, despite Vince and me being there.

"What about school?" Margaret asked.

"I can still go to school, *Mom*."

I couldn't see Margaret's face, but given her tone, I was sure she wasn't smiling.

"This is what you want?"

Tammy nodded. "I'm cashing in my plane ticket. We're going to get his car fixed and drive out."

"Vincent, are you sure this is what you need to do, how you want to handle this?"

There was a change in her tone as Margaret continued interrogating them, from surprised to concern, and then to acceptance. Vince's eyes lowered, and the tension in the room grew. He was ashamed to be in this situation, to have the girls know, but there was no escaping it now. His broken voice cut right through me and sealed our fate. "I have to get out of here."

Chapter 14 - Margaret

SOME COUPLES BOND OVER conversation. Some manage to do it in silence, letting unspoken emotions seal their fate. For William and me, it would be stealing a car.

"It's not stealing. The Nova belongs to Vince."

I didn't feel any better about it. We were sitting down the street from Vincent's house, waiting for the lights to go out and his father to go to bed.

"It's going to be trouble if his dad catches us."

William shook his head. "As soon as you drop me off, go to my house and wait for me there."

"Are you sure you're going to be able to drive it?"

William shot me a look. "It's just the clutch. As long as I watch the RPMs, it'll fall into gear without it if I time it right."

"How are you going to start it without the clutch?"

William sighed, ignoring my question. "I don't want to keep you out here any longer than I have to. Drop me off and go on. I'm going to try and roll it into the street. Hopefully, he's asleep, but if he's not, at least we'll be gone before he realizes what's happening."

"Try? What happens if you can't?"

"I can do it. Whatever you do, don't sit at the end of the driveway, 'cause when I go, I'm going. Got it?"

"Got it." My belly was a mess of nerves. I should have been home hours ago. Instead, I was sitting on the street in Tammy's parent's car because William's stood out too much, waiting to steal another one. How did I get here?

"He's going to bed."

I looked up. The lights had gone out in the house. My anxiety soared.

"I'll push it out into the street and start it." William nodded at the road ahead of us, pointing out the slope. "I can change the gears once I get rolling, or I'll wake up the whole damn neighborhood when they start grinding."

I felt my face go pale. William didn't miss my sudden distress and winked. "I got this. We'll give him a few minutes to get settled and then we'll go."

Nodding, despite that William's attention was back on the house, I wondered for a moment why Vincent hadn't just called his dad and told him William was coming to get the car. Images of Mr. Bradford confronting William quickly derailed the train of thought. If he was that brutal with his own son, how violent would he get with William?

Finally, William said, "Let's go." Pulling the car into the street, I passed Vincent's house and pulled over a few driveways down.

"I'm not leaving until I know you're good. I'll go down the street and get out of your way, but I'm falling in behind you to make sure you get home."

William flashed me a smile. If I didn't know any better, I'd think he was proud. He leaned over, gave me a quick kiss and left the car.

As promised, I pulled down to where the slope of the road leveled out and started an uphill climb, but close enough that I could see when William made it into the street. We were counting on the keys being in the car where Vincent said he'd left them. If his dad had gotten them, it would be a whole new game.

The minutes ticked by. More than once the mass of nerves in my stomach threatened to come up. Checking the side mirror, again, I swallowed the urge to vomit. God, strike me down if I ever do something like this again. My nerves couldn't stand it. What was taking him so long?

Finally, the car eased out of the driveway, coming to a quiet stop in the street. For a heartbeat, there was no activity, and then the car lurched forward and the engine roared to life. There was a brief echo of metal against metal in the night and then the car accelerated. The headlights came on, and I pulled the shifter into drive, pulling into the street behind William.

At the top of the hill, William slowed and turned right against the light without stopping while I held my breath and prayed no one was coming. When he cleared the intersection without getting hit, I let go a sigh of relief. I made the turn, not surprised to see the tail lights from Vincent's car way down the street. Following behind, I drove safely, letting the distance between us grow. William had it under control, and I began to relax, convincing myself that it wasn't such a bad thing we'd done. Vincent was grown, but even I could see he'd always be considered Bradford's failed son. He needed to get away from here, out of this town.

The garage at William's house set over to the side of the property, a converted carriage house from days gone by. He was waiting outside, propped against the door, when I pulled in, looking every bit like the rebel he was. I stepped out of the car, leaning my hip against the fender.

"We're going to have to work on your driving, Marguerite."

I grinned in spite of my nerves; relief and self-consciousness flooded my body. Why did this man affect me like this? He eased toward me, his arms crossed. His lazy stride was confident, and his presence consumed me. I was frozen in place and easy prey.

"Are you going to let me take the Shelby racing?" My squeaky question brought a smile to William's face. Christ, I could barely speak.

"Is that what you want to do?" William raised his eyebrow, amused.

"No." My hesitation gave me away. He leaned his head to the side, silently calling me out on my answer. He was on me now, in my space and stealing my reality.

"Maybe."

His look of amusement grew into a grin. "And here I thought you were such a good girl."

"I am."

With his face just inches from me, William diverted a kiss to my cheek. "I just bet you are."

With his eyes on me, he pulled away and headed for the driver's seat. "You coming?"

There was that smug smile again. I was cheated. I wanted more. A kiss. Something more than a peck on the cheek. He'd walked away because he'd known I wanted more. He was taunting me, torturing me. How was I going to survive him?

Chapter 15 - William

I THINK THE SEXIEST thing I'd ever seen was Margaret in jeans and my old t-shirt with grease smeared across her face. "Replace this hose with that one," was all I had to tell her. She would search through the tools, find what she needed for the clamps and then she did it. All I had to do was check behind her to make sure they were tight enough and point out the next one.

She'd come over after she'd left her babysitting job, offering to help get Vince's car ready for their trip. I hadn't expected her to be more than company. Company I was happy to have, but she dove right in, grease and all. She always seemed to surprise me.

When the hoses were done, we moved on to replacing the spark plugs, wires, and belts. We worked for hours and not once did Margaret complain. Finished, I looked at her and wiped a smudge of grease from her cheek. With my own dirty hands, it only served to make it worse. "You want to go to the house and get cleaned up?"

The workshop didn't have running water, but there was a hose outside the building if she didn't want to go in.

"I'm really not ready for the whole meeting of the parents moment right now, William."

She stood, her arms spread; her nose wrinkled and looking absolutely adorable. I pulled her into me wondering how I'd gotten so lucky. Her in my arms. This was life. Exactly what I wanted my life to be.

"Just means I have you to myself a little longer." I picked her up and sat her on the car.

"You think they're going to be all right?"

"Tammy and Vince?"

"Mhm."

That delicate stretch of skin on her neck had gotten my attention again, and Margaret seemed less and less interested in conversation as I worked my way up. I pulled her hips to me and eased her down on the hood. By the time I reached her lips, her fingers were tangled in my hair, and her crotch was pressed into my hard on.

My hands journeyed down her ribs to the hem of her shirt. I eased my hands up, bringing her shirt with them. My lips left hers for her chin, her throat. I moved to her exposed belly and trailed my tongue to the waist of her jeans, tugging at the button with my teeth.

"William."

My mother. Fucking Christ. I stood, pulling Margaret's shirt down. Her moan of frustration with my departure brought a smile to my face.

"William, Vincent's on the phone."

She was calling again. "She's going to come in here if I don't go." I reached for her hand and pulled her up. "I'll be back in a few minutes."

"What's he going to do when he gets there?"

Margaret leaned against Vince's car, crossing her arms like Vince was going to cause Tammy's dreams to implode. There was no going back to where we'd left off. Damn phone.

"Get a job, I guess. He's smart. Smarter than people think."

"Much like you're nicer than people think?"

I couldn't help but laugh. "You think I'm nice?" I was fishing for a compliment, but I didn't care. Her eyes met mine, and she nodded.

"I know so."

I wanted to cross the short distance between us and take the kiss I wanted so badly, to pick up where we left off. *Not yet.* The little voice in the back of my mind was heard over the temptation washing through me. Wouldn't the town find it amusing, William Steele, going out of his way to keep his hands *off* a girl?

Margaret was worried about her friend and it wasn't the time. Grinning at how life works out, I pushed up from that rickety stool where I'd been sitting. "I should probably take you home."

Margaret pushed herself off the car. "I could use a bath."

I let us out of the shop and opened the passenger door to the Shelby. "When do I get a do-over for dinner?" Her easy laugh rolled from the car.

"Saturday, William."

Slamming the door shut, I went around and climbed in. "Saturday it is."

Chapter 16 - Margaret

EVEN THE MINIATURE MONSTERS couldn't spoil my mood during the week. It flew by while I mentally surrounded myself with happy thoughts and let their constant squabbling bounce off me. Mr. Anderson had seemed a little perturbed all week. He finally told me today that Mrs. Anderson was coming home Saturday, and they were going to make a go of it again. Good riddance and farewell. I was happy to grab my cash and escape the house.

Tammy was sitting on the porch with something on her mind when I got home. She smiled as I approached, standing to hug me. I sat down on the steps, and Tammy took a seat beside me.

"You're leaving, aren't you?"

"Margaret, I never meant to deceive you about Vince. I tried not to care about him. I didn't see a future for us. It got complicated quick."

"Now you do?"

Tammy nodded. "I've had such a snobbish attitude." She laid her head on my shoulder. "I always thought the bruises were because he was a troublemaker, getting into fights. He's had 'em his whole life." Her voice was thick with unshed tears. "I just can't believe all this."

"I thought the same thing. I can't believe you never told Vincent you were going to law school. He seemed surprised about that." The two didn't compare, but I felt the need to lighten the mood.

Tammy groaned. "It's gotten so complicated, Margaret. I never thought it would matter."

I rested my cheek against her hair. I couldn't imagine Vincent's life either. It had sort of slapped me in the face, but come hell or high water, I was going to do what I could to help him get away from here.

"When are you leaving?"

"Vince talked to William earlier this week about everything he'd need. If we can get his car tuned up and ready to go, Monday morning. It's still a little hard for him to move around."

Tammy couldn't see my face or the huge smile I was wearing. So, that's what the phone call had been about. She'd be shocked to know William and I had the car ready.

"He still at the hotel?"

"Yes."

"You sure about this, Tammy?"

She nodded, her hair tickling my face.

"I can't believe I never caught on."

"I'm sorry I never told you. I know it seems stupid, but I thought you'd stop hanging out with me if you knew I was hanging out with him. Besides, it was never meant to go this far. Now look, you're hanging out with William Steele. I about fell out of the booth when he sat down beside you at the diner."

"We weren't hanging out then," I corrected her.

After spending time around William, Tammy's language barely fazed me and her excuse was flimsy, but the truth was, a month ago, those guys scared me to death. I could see her point. "Wait here." I kissed her head and stood, going inside. I retrieved what I needed and raced back down the stairs.

"Take this with you." I handed Tammy the folded bills, ignoring her wide-eyed surprise.

"Margaret, I can't take this."

I pushed the money back toward her. "You can. I've been saving for school. I won't need it."

"But your mom?"

I sat back down, ignoring Tammy's attempt to give the money back. "They aren't going to take money from me. You guys are going to have to live somewhere. You'll need food. What if his car breaks down? Take it. It's not that much, but it'll help until he finds a job."

Tammy collapsed beside me on the porch. "I'll pay you back. Every dime, Margaret."

"With interest, when the time is right." I hugged her to me, sad to be letting my best friend go, but this just felt right.

At five minutes to six I heard a car pull into the driveway. A huge smile grew on my face, answering the doubts and questions about whether he would show. I went to the door and pulled it open as William stepped onto the porch. He was handsome, dressed in jeans and a button down, white, collared shirt. His hair shined in the evening sun, but it was wind-blown, despite his efforts to smooth it down. I tamped my smile down to a grin. "Hey."

William looked around with a nervous grin on his face. "Do I need to come in?" He shoved his hands into the pocket of his jeans as he waited, looking a little less confident. After the last time he and my father had gotten together, I can't say I blame him, but it was cute. I bit back a smile at how hard he was working to hide his nervousness. The realization helped to soothe my own.

"No, we're fine. Dad is working, and Mom is resting." I left it at that, and William stood aside, waiting while I locked up the house. "Where are we going?"

"Where would you like to go?" he countered.

The reality was, there wasn't much to choose from except the diner without driving to the next town. That put us at risk of running into Victoria. If she wasn't there, a crowd of other people William hung out with would be.

He eyed me carefully. "The joy of small town living, huh?"

"Well, I won't live here forever, so I may as well enjoy it while I can." Enthusiasm was hard to fake. "We could ask the diner to box up something for us, if you want, take it back to the park, maybe? Or back to the lake."

"You wouldn't mind that?" William asked.

"Let me run in and get a blanket."

Minutes later we were headed to the diner, the silence feeding the tension with each passing block. William may have known whether Victoria would be there or not, but I didn't, and I didn't want to ask. Way too soon we were pulling into the crowded parking lot. This felt different than the couple of times we'd ran into each other here. This was a *date*. What would his friends say about him showing up with me?

There was little time to dwell on it before William was opening my door and taking my hand. He helped me out of the car, wrapped his arm around me and eased me into the diner, acknowledging his friends and holding me to him like it was the most natural thing in the world. If William Steele was embarrassed to be seen on a date with me, it didn't show.

We took a seat at the counter, and I scanned the dining area for Victoria. It was busy. Customers crammed the sleek red vinyl booths, squeezed in some three and four deep. Scattered among them were the empty tables, littered with debris and waiting for someone to clean it up and wipe it down for the next group. Several waitresses hurried amongst the tables, but Victoria was nowhere to be seen.

It took a few minutes before Regina could get to us. She looked from me to William, not bothering to hide her disapproval.

"What can I get you?"

I rambled off my usual cheeseburger with the works and an order of fries. When I was done, Regina turned her body to William, but never raised her gaze to meet him. With his head slightly bowed, eyeing her with a degree of irritation at her slight, he added his choices behind mine. While we waited, William turned his stool toward me, watching me intently while I rubbed my fingers across the Formica counter top.

"I should have thought this through, better," he admitted.

I forced a smiled, turning my attention to him, staring at those cute little parentheses that emphasized his lips. Why did my attention always seem to gravitate there? "It's OK. It's one date."

"One date, huh?" His eyes clouded over, and he leaned into me. "I've hung out. I've gotten laid. I haven't done dates. If it goes to shit, I get a do-over. It's automatic."

I leaned away from his confident explanation. "I think we need to get through this one date and see how traumatized you are. Your ego may not hold up so well with rejection."

Despite my playful smile, my face heated at the subtle meaning, but I felt it was important for William to know that I would not be shedding my skirt for him, or any other man except my future husband. His moves in the garage had overwhelmed me; it was all so new. Now, I was prepared. It seemed people all over the planet were spreading as much love, peace and happiness as they could stand, but I didn't think sharing my body without love would bring much peace or happiness.

His eyebrows shot up, but his face remained gentle and soft, completely devoid of mischievousness, almost regretful. "You must think I'm the devil, Marguerite."

"I think you're a victim of society's judgment. But, just in case I'm wrong, I want you to know where I stand." I softened the blow with a smile and was rewarded with a subtle dip of William's head.

"Fair enough." He eyed me for a moment, his brown eyes searching. "You seem nervous. You've been alone with me before."

"Tuning up Vincent's car wasn't a date."

"Sure felt like one." William's features twisted into a knowing look, and I knew exactly what he was remembering: me sprawled on the hood of Vincent's car.

"Does it really make a difference?"

In my mind it did. We had a focus, a project. This was a date and expectations were different.

Regina returned with our food, and William collected the bags, threw some money on the counter, and we stood to leave, making our way through the maze of tables. Before we could make it to the doors, Victoria breezed in with Anthony in tow.

She noticed William and froze. I stepped closer to him, sealing any doubt she may have that he was there alone. Her eyes widened, and her lips pulled back, revealing just about every tooth in her mouth. "So it *is* true."

Her body twitched in muffled chuckles before a full-blown fit of laughter washed over her. "Good luck with that," she squealed. Her attention was back on William, but she was pointing at me. I stepped into her line of vision, forcing her to look at me. Despite the heat warming my cheeks, I straightened my small frame and still managed to come in several inches shorter than her. Anthony had made a wide berth around us and moved on to the counter, giving Victoria a hateful look, but leaving her to fend for herself. If she wasn't so mean, I think I would have felt sorry for her. But, she was, and I didn't.

"I would say William's luck has improved," I countered. "It's the difference between bedding and breeding, Victoria. You know, like a whore and a housewife?"

William's presence invaded my space, but I kept my attention on Victoria, giving her a chance to respond.

"You had better watch your back," she hissed, cutting her eyes from William back to me.

William's hands landed on my shoulders. "That's my job."

Victoria stepped back, her sneer transforming into a placating smile. A second later she snorted and walked away as William and I stood united against her. When his hands dropped from my shoulders, I turned, waited for him to pick up the food he'd set aside, and together we walked back to his car. William barely made it outside before the laughter he'd been holding back roared free.

"Who'd have thought that little Miss Fucking Margaret Wilson would stand like a stone?"

"Your language is atrocious," I said, flatly.

Instead of apologizing, William shrugged and eyed me with a rebellious grin and winked. I couldn't help but smile.

Chapter 17 - William

MARGARET SHRUGGED OFF MY compliment, so I started the car and replayed in my mind what had just happened. Not Victoria's behavior, but the pride I felt when Margaret stood up to her. She didn't go psycho bitch and start pulling hair or stand there trading insults like school kids. Margaret said her piece, calling Vicky a whore in the nicest way possible and still managed to make her speechless. I was impressed that, not only did she do it, but she did it with style.

My grin grew. I think I'm in love. I propped my elbow on the door and rested my head on my fist as I drove. How exactly did I get from there to here, from fucking Vicky wherever the chance came to us, to not only having a picnic in a park but having barely thought past what would happen when I saw Margaret again. Hell, I was just excited to see her.

"I'm sure that was unpleasant. What do we do now?"

"What? No, it wasn't unpleasant at all. I like seeing you all steamed up."

I risked a glance to see my date eyeing me with some caution. "Come on, Margaret. She's probably never been stood up to in her whole life. That's why her parents can't reign her in now." I chuckled at the memory of the tiny woman beside me, chin up, defiant and pretty much calling Vicky a whore, unworthy of being a housewife.

I reached over and took her hand in mine. "We're going to go and eat our dinner and have a good time."

"You're rebounding."

I sighed. I could tell it was bothering her, and I didn't want to brush off her feelings. "Maybe she needed to go so you could come."

Margaret rolled her eyes at my emphasis on *come* before turning away, but she couldn't hide the rosy blush creeping up her neck. Little Miss Margaret may not be willing to do the deed, but she'd given some thought to it. I was sure of it.

"Seriously, though. Maybe I needed to make room for you in my life. Have you thought about that?" I asked, trying to keep the conversation on track. The shy hesitation that continued to color her face made it hard to turn away. I had no intention of pushing Margaret, but it sure made me happy to see her respond like that. It was exactly that reason I couldn't stop.

Margaret was quiet for a moment. "No, but *you* obviously have."

I dipped my head to agree. "I've thought of little but you." The honest statement rolled off my tongue too easy. I waited for a rebuff, but the only response was her fingers tightening around mine.

We drove the rest of the way in silence. At the park, Margaret grabbed the blanket while I got the food. We found a spot in a grove of trees that was pushed back from the play area and was relatively quiet.

"Doesn't it bother you?" Margaret was separating our order as she spoke.

"What?"

"Moving on so quickly."

Margaret unfolded her burger from the greasy wax paper, taking a moment to bless her food.

I waited quietly for her to finish her blessing, wondering why her comment stabbed at me. How could I make her see how little Vicky meant to me without sounding like a jerk? I snapped off a bite of my burger, giving the irritation a chance to simmer down. What kind of person did she think I was?

Maybe that was the problem. She knew exactly who I was, but there was a difference in the man I was and the man she made me want to be. I swallowed down the burger before I'd chewed it well enough, unable to wait any longer.

"No, we had fun while it lasted. It's time for something else, something different. Something better. Besides, she's the one who cheated."

"Yes, but if she hadn't cheated, you'd still be together."

I sighed, growing agitated at the direction of this conversation. "You think too much, Margaret."

To her credit, she didn't even flinch, but she remained quiet for a moment, eating her food and pretending to be lost in checking out the park. "You go through girls like water."

I chuckled at her observation. "Have you ever even been kissed, Margaret? Aside from me?"

The question threw her off-track, but she quickly recovered. "Of course I have."

I didn't think she was lying, but the way she popped a fry in her mouth led me to think she didn't want to discuss it. She swallowed, saying, "You're avoiding the elephant, again."

I crossed my legs and turned to her. "OK, this is bothering you. Let's talk and get it out of the way." I took a sip from my Coke, set it to the side and clasped my hands in front of me. "You would never be dumped like Vicky because you won't behave like Vicky. Period. End of story."

"Being dumped implies we're together."

Damn her analytical mind. I wanted to move this date forward. "Aren't we? If I punched Anthony Beckman for kissing Vicky, you can damn well believe I'd beat someone's ass over you." I didn't stop to think we'd only hung out a few times. It was irrelevant. It seemed like weeks already and besides, Margaret Wilson was different. She was the day to my night. Good to my bad. She was the complete opposite of everything I was and had been, and that's exactly why I wanted her.

"Calm down. I'm just curious about the appeal of it, William. Why bounce from one girl to another like you're trying out a bicycle? Some would claim you can't be loyal. Or won't be. I don't want that."

I shook my head. "There are only a few people in my life who deserve my loyalty and, I assure you, they have it, completely."

She dipped her head in a subtle nod. "And you're OK with my parent's limitations?"

Laughing at her question, I spun around, laying my head beside where she sat. Since the night she'd came to the hotel, she hadn't seemed all that concerned about her parent's rules. The perfect daughter was slipping. "I've never negotiated to get a girlfriend before."

"I've not heard the rumor that you've kept a girlfriend before."

She was laughing, and I covered my face in mock shame, but if she were willing to let Vicky go, I'd take it. "Rub it in, Marguerite."

"Maybe I'm not girlfriend material, William." Her hand landed on my forehead and seconds later her fingers were raking through my hair.

I thought back to what she'd said to Vicky. "No, you're more wife material," I breathed.

Chapter 18 – Margaret

WILLIAM SETTLED BACK ON the blanket, the conversation about Vicky and his womanizing habits settled. I hated to sound so insecure about it all, but I could see myself standing alone in the near future, crying over that moment he broke my heart. Last Saturday was explained, but the horrible pain that had come with it at the time had been new, unbearable, and I didn't ever want to feel that disappointment again.

"Does who I am bother you?"

I wasn't sure how to answer that. Everything inside of me told me William wasn't the person the world saw him as. Yes, he was a bit of a rebel. He raced cars on the streets, balked at rules and seemed to live his life the way he wanted to. Was he any worse than half the other men in this world his age? He also seemed to be honest and upfront so, to me, it lifted him to a level higher than most.

"No."

He peered up at me as if to see if I was serious or not. He must have been satisfied. He settled back down and closed his eyes again.

"Why are your parents so strict? Don't they trust you?"

"Of course. It's people like you *they* don't trust." William took my joking in stride. I thought of the Anderson children. "In all seriousness, kids need boundaries."

William rolled to his side, bringing his face within inches of mine. "Do you push those boundaries, Marguerite?"

"No."

"Why?" he asked, tilting his head.

His invasion of my space stole my breath. I waited, watching him, hoping for a kiss that never came. Instead, he remained inches away, creating a tension between us and allowing it to soar until I couldn't take it anymore.

"Are you going to kiss me?" I felt like a little girl who'd just handed her playground crush a check-yes-or-no love note. Giddy. Scared. Excited.

"Nope." William retreated, lying down again and folding his arms under his head and gazing up at the darkening sky.

"Why?" I asked, trying to keep the disappointment from my voice.

"Because I like the idea of you kissing me."

William turned his face toward me. "Are *you* OK with that?"

Something in the way he looked at me sparked a challenge, his brown eyes, serious and wide with expectation, his lips pulled to the side. I was drawn to him, and we met in a kiss so soft I barely felt the warmth of his lips. I inched from him, but William wrapped his free hand into my hair and stopped me. This time, held by him, my lips pressed against his until I could feel his breath warm and caress my face.

This was different than in the breezeway. The same cocky approach, but then I was in shock, too confused and tired and surprised to think about it. Now, my mind raced to commit this moment to memory. My body flushed with heat; my heart was pounding in my chest. A shiver of disappointment ran through my body when he released me, running his tongue over his bottom lip. "Can't do too much of that," he finally breathed.

I cleared my throat, wanting more of the same. Instead, I went back to my food while William toyed with his. We finished eating in silence, me pondering the wave of indecency that William's kiss had set off inside me. He was watching me with a self-satisfied smirk as if he knew the emotions his kiss had me sorting out. This had been nothing like when Peter Simpkins stole a kiss at the water fountain my sophomore year or even the sloppy, wet kiss I'd gotten from Timothy Andrews after the last football game.

I finished my fries, wiped my hands and lay down to face William on the blanket. "Tell me about you."

William rolled his eyes in disgust. "There isn't much this place doesn't know about me."

"No, there's not much this place doesn't *assume* about you. There's a difference," I corrected. "I know that your driving skills suck. I'm not sure I believe all these racing rumors. Your ability to hold on to a girlfriend is even less impressive, and you've been known for fighting."

Despite our proximity, William's gaze ventured right, avoiding mine. He rolled to his back and slid his hands beneath his head, again. "It's hard to explain, Margaret. Everyone in this town thinks they know me, my family. They tell their kids, and the kids make my life shit, always have. Being rich may be great in places where there are a lot of other rich people, but in a town like this, it singles you out, makes you a target. Instead of being part of an elite pack, the regular kids are the pack, and you become their target, all because their grandparents told their parents things that aren't true or that happened fifty years ago."

I rolled over on my back and gave his words some thought. It was true. It was a small town, and there was nowhere to hide your secrets.

The church was the biggest building in our town. Religion was a powerful staple here and in our home, as important as food and shelter, and my short life had revolved around the Bible and its teachings. Perception was everything. Yet, here I was, lying on a blanket in the middle of a park with the worst bad boy in town.

"What's on your mind, Marguerite?"

"I'm thinking I don't much like living here."

"You're done with school. What's your plan?"

I sighed. "I haven't thought about it. My mother is sick; my father works too much. I don't think too far ahead, William." It was an abbreviated version of the truth. I didn't want to share with him that there wasn't enough money in the family coffers to send me to college. Besides, it was the worst possible time to think of leaving home.

"What's wrong with your mother?"

There was genuine concern in his voice and despite the fact that I barely knew him, hadn't we just committed ourselves to each other? Besides, with Tammy leaving, my best friend moments would become nonexistent. I could use the friend.

"Her kidneys," I explained. "They're doing what they can, but..." I couldn't bring myself to say the words. I could feel the tears gather in the corner of my eyes, and I blinked, willing them away before he noticed. I liked William. A lot. Maybe I shouldn't have burdened him with so much information.

"Isn't there a treatment?"

I nodded in the growing darkness. "Yes, but there are so many sick people that need treatment. Too many. It's a textbook example of a failure in supply versus demand," I added, cynically. "The committee denied her."

"Committee?"

"There's a group of people who pick and choose who gets dialysis and who doesn't."

"You mean a group who decides who lives and who dies?" he asked softly. When I didn't answer, he said, "If it were my wife, I'd be raising hell until they gave in or I went to prison."

I glanced over to see him looking up at the sky, watching the last of the clouds disappear as the inky dark spread, wiping out the last of the red and blues of the sunset. I should have taken offense at the underlying tone that my father shouldn't stop short of violence to save his wife. But, that was his nature. He wrote relentlessly to Congress, to local and state medical boards, outlining, begging them to reconsider treatment options, not just for my mother, but the masses of those who were left with only palliative care. He worked all the overtime he could to pay for doctors and everything that came with them.

"I have no doubt that you'd storm the seven levels of hell to save her."

"You."

"I'm sorry?" I heard him, but my mind wasn't quite wrapping around what he'd said.

"It will be you." William enunciated the words carefully, and I bit back the giggle of such a romantic notion coming from him.

William reached out to me, and I found myself snuggled against him, my head resting on his chest and his arms wrapped around me.

"You are completely unaware of yourself, Margaret. You've no idea the draw you have, and I don't understand why, in a town this small, I haven't met you already."

"Maybe things would have been different if you'd gone to school with us." I tried lightening the tone. William may not have known me, but I'd known who he was for years. Everyone did. It was impossible in this town not to know the Steele family, even if the hierarchy of the town kept them from knowing you.

"I went to the county schools for a while," he said. "I was young — real young. Things were rough." His tone told me they weren't pleasant memories. "Private schools will often overlook things as long as the tuition is paid, but the teachers don't have to like it."

I thought I understood. If the kids were cruel and got their information from the adults, the teachers couldn't be much better than the ruthless children. Even some of them couldn't have been immune to the Steele legacy and probably singled him out just as much as the children had.

"Now you're avoiding the elephant. Where do you want to go? And don't give me that 'I haven't thought about it,' crap. Everyone has, even in crisis."

He was right, of course. I had thought of little else up until the day I realized my mother would never get any better. I took a moment to organize my thoughts. "I don't care where I go, as long as it's outside of town, outside of civilization. I suffocate here."

"A house in the country?"

My smile said it all, but those were dreams. Big, expensive dreams.

"Tell me what you want."

I thought back over the visions of my childhood, the giant house I had dreamed of. I shared this with William. "And a sprawling yard with trees for shade in the summer where I can sit and read the day away. I need a swing for four just off of a shady spot where all my children can play."

"*Our* children," William corrected me. "I don't know why you keep leaving me out of *our* future."

I giggled at his optimism but ignored his input. "I want a giant kitchen. I love to cook, with a refrigerator full of vegetables and a counter full of cake."

William laughed. "A complete contradiction."

"What do you want, William?"

Chapter 19 - William

INSPIRED BY MARGARET, MY dreams picked up where hers left off. "I want to learn everything I can about my father's business. I want to be a man my…our…children will be proud of. I want to give you all those things you just mentioned, including a giant bed in that giant house sitting on a sprawling yard to make all those beautiful children we're going to have."

She laughed.

"And I'd like you to kiss me again."

Her laugh faded into silence. "I'd like that, too," she whispered.

Under the cover of darkness, with just the glow of the moon lighting her face, without much thought at all, I rolled over, pinning Margaret half under the weight of my body. Her lips parted, stunned, but she didn't push me away.

"William," she breathed, and whether I imagined it or not, there seemed to be a rush of excitement in her whisper.

I leaned in and brushed my tongue against her lips, pausing to give her a chance to object. Instead, she raised her head, meeting me in the tiny space between us, and my fate was sealed.

Moments later, when I was able to pull myself away, I stood and offered Margaret my hand. This really was dangerous territory and lying on this blanket, alone in the park, I couldn't trust myself. Given Margaret's enthusiasm for our kiss, I couldn't trust her to keep me in my place, either.

She took my hand and allowed me to pull her to her feet. "I should take you home."

Without a word, she gathered the trash from our supper, and I took it and put it in a nearby receptacle, grateful for the night, the darkness that hid my arousal. Margaret folded the blanket and pulled it to her chest, wrapping her arms around it, hugging it to her. We started walking back to the car, and I shoved my hands in my pocket, the silence suddenly awkward. I was determined to do right by Margaret, yet I could tell from the look on her face that her disappointment was weighing on her.

"Are we having our first tiff?" Margaret asked as we approached the passenger side door. She pulled herself up to stand before me, her eyes wet with unshed tears. I'd handled this all wrong.

"No," I stammered. A single tear slid down her cheek, and it was my undoing. I collapsed against the car, running my hands through my hair, tangling the strands around my fingers and pulling in frustration. "Margaret, I'm trying here."

"I told you I wasn't your kind of girl, William. I can't do this. I don't want to learn to love you only to lose you."

My heart dropped with her confession. I barely knew her, but I knew she was the woman who would stand behind me, she was the crutch that would help me stand taller, be better than I was. Everything I saw and felt was different, more vibrant and real when I was with her. I had to protect that.

"This has nothing to do with losing me, Margaret. This is about me losing myself in you and forgetting all the things I promised myself I wouldn't do." I risked a look at Margaret. "The things you wanted to wait to do."

I wrapped my arms around her and pulled her to me. "I feel like I'll ruin you." I laughed nervously at my fumbled explanation. The truth was this woman in my arms exuded a goodness that had never touched my life before, like all that was good in the world was contained in her tiny body just drawing others to her light. Was I worthy of this? If I wasn't, I would become so.

"I've disappointed you." The tremble in her voice took me by surprise.

"What? Why would you say that? No."

"Because you jumped up, ready to take me home like you always do. I'm sorry I can't be like all the other girls; it's just not me."

The laugh erupted without warning. "Margaret, you've came pretty fucking close a couple of times, but if you were like all the other girls, I wouldn't want only you."

I felt her body swell with a deep breath and the slow collapse of her shoulders as she exhaled. "Margaret, I just can't touch you and not want to touch you more. It's not a disappointment thing, it's a, *you're hot and I want you* thing."

"You think I'm hot?" She looked up at me, a playful smile tugging at her lips.

"Ten minutes ago, I could have shown you, in a big way, how hot I think you are."

It took a moment, but her eyes widened when she realized my meaning. I hugged her back to me and grinned into the night. It was going to be a fine line, but being with Margaret was going to be one hell of a ride.

Chapter 20 - Margaret

WE LINGERED AT THE car a little longer, letting the tension from the moment work itself out. I hated being intimidated by this. It was all so new, but the glimpse of disappointment I had last week was still fresh.

William took me home and walked me to the gate, leaving me with a chaste kiss on my cheek. He took off in his Shelby, racing off down the road in the direction of his house.

Monday afternoon he picked me up at and we drove to the hotel to say goodbye to Tammy and Vincent. His car was packed with her things, but there was very little that Vincent had bothered to retrieve from his house.

"I can't believe you did all this." Vincent looked at me, waving his hand at his car.

"I didn't help that much."

Tammy was throwing her arms around me before I finished. "You've done too much. My parents may never talk to you again."

I laughed because I couldn't find the words. I'd known Tammy since I could walk and I had known she was going off to school, yet now that that day was here, I wasn't ready.

"That's OK. I only hung around because of you." My voice was tight with emotion and Tammy squeezed me a little tighter before releasing me.

William was quick to step into her place, wrapping his arm around me as he offered his free hand to Vincent. They shook, and Tammy eased her arms around Vincent's still sore body. The swelling was better on his face, but the bruises were just starting to fade, and I was sure the rest of him was still recuperating.

"You guys be safe," William said. "I don't plan on going to LA to kick anyone's ass."

"Man, you're not going to have to. But if you do, Miss Lawyer will have your back. I will, too."

"That's years down the road," Tammy said, gently patting his chest. "We better get going."

Another quick hug between Tammy and me and they were gone. William pulled me back into his arms as the Nova disappeared around the corner.

"You all right?"

I nodded, letting out a long breath. "I hope they know what they're doing."

William turned me toward the hotel. "I don't think anybody would have changed their mind. They'll be fine. Maybe not together, but they're both tough; they'll be all right."

I giggled at William's take on things. He was right, of course. Tammy was strong; I knew she'd be fine in California. Poor Vincent was leaving the only life he'd known, as bad as it was. I'd have to take William's word on him.

We went to the room, and William slipped the key in the door. I followed in behind him, not knowing if this was a good idea or not. William pulled me inside, shutting the door behind us. I found myself pinned between him and the door, his eyes blazing into mine.

"The room is paid up."

What was I supposed to say to that? My eyes drifted past him to the bed and William's lips curved into a suggestive smile. "I thought we might could watch some TV."

Disappointment offset the excitement racing through me just a second ago. "Watch TV?"

William nodded. "Unless you have something else on your mind."

He was watching me, that familiar smirk playing on his lips. I shook my head, but my eyes once again drifted to the bed like it was a force of nature. "TV is fine."

He pushed away, allowing the air in the room to return to my space. I closed my eyes. Not even a kiss. "Damn."

Jesus. My eyes flew open to see William looking at me, his head tilted with a questioning look on his face. "Did you just cuss?"

I opened my mouth, but the words were frozen in my throat. I swallowed, but my saliva seemed to have dried up. The way he was looking at me. I was in trouble. "I'm grown." It was a weak defense.

William straightened his head and seemed to be physically pulling himself together. "Are you now?"

He was retracing his steps, stalking his way back to me. I couldn't look at him. A hundred thoughts were racing through me, and none of them were appropriate. As soon as he was in reach, he cupped my chin in his hand, raising my face to him. This wasn't my tender *I'm not going to rush you*, William. This was the William of every girl's dream. And I wanted him.

Somewhere in-between William kissing me and my body molding to his, we found ourselves on the bed. My heart was beating so loudly in my ears it took me a minute to realize the sound echoing through the room wasn't coming from inside me.

"Fucking shit." William groaned, rolling off me. His feet hit the floor and seconds later he swung open the door.

"Is this what's become of you, Margaret?"

My father stood there, his face so irate you could see the pulse throbbing in his temple. I jumped from the bed, my arms hugging my still clothed body. "Daddy, what are you doing here?"

He looked past William. "You're supposed to be with your mother. Mrs. Ramone called and said she's been throwing up for the last hour."

I was so ashamed standing there. "How did you know I was here?" I asked, looking at the floor. "Is mom OK?"

"No, she is not OK, you know this, and I find you here. With *him*."

I instinctively took a step back as he spat the words. William took a step in my direction. I held up my hand, stopping him.

"I'm taking her to the hospital. I thought you might like to know."

"I'll go with you," I said, moving toward the door.

My dad shook his head. "I don't think it's a good idea for me to be around you right now. I just had to see it for myself."

With that, my father turned and left. I stood, trembling, almost oblivious to William pulling me into his arms. I couldn't believe my father had just left me like that. That he had talked to me that way and turned his back on me. I knew my mother was sick. That's why I asked Mrs. Ramone to check on her. The familiar sting of tears in my eyes was becoming an all too familiar feeling.

"I'm sorry, Margaret. He's just afraid." William's voice was soft, but what did he know of my family and me? I was a disgrace.

He was still my father, and he still supported me, and I still owed it to him to act in a way that reflected well on him and my mother. I separated myself from William and absently smoothed my hair down as I eased toward the door. I'd known William a month. What was I thinking?

"I'm sorry, William. I have to go." I couldn't bring myself to look him in the face. I was humiliated. This was not the girl I was raised to be.

"Margaret." William had caught my elbow before I reached the open door. I collapsed into his arms with a deep breath that still left me needing more. I would lose him after this—over this.

I felt his lips leave a firm kiss on my hair, and I pulled myself from him. "I have to go."

Chapter 21 - William

I STOOD AT THE door long after Margaret was gone. Having a hard time wrapping my head around the Margaret I knew with the Margaret that had just walked out of here, I was confused, and a pit of uneasiness had grown in my gut. Pushing the door shut, I collapsed onto the bed.

That had gone from sugar to shit in three seconds flat. I really had intended on watching TV. That demure fucking look on Margaret's face after she'd cussed was like a damn stroke of insanity for me. I scratched my palms across my face. *This*. This was fucking insanity.

Jumping up, I headed for the door, fishing my keys from my pocket. It might be a Monday night, but it was the middle of summer and there'd be a party somewhere.

There was a pack of cars parked at the diner, and I eased the Shelby into a parking spot off to the side. I hopped out, catching the random hands that reached out to me in smooth greetings.

"What's up tonight?"

I barely had my ass on the picnic table before she jumped in my lap. My arms went around her to keep her from falling through my knees and landing on the pavement. "Whoa, what have you been into tonight?"

Tabitha's arms slithered around my neck and the smell of cheap perfume surrounded me as her wet whisper sprayed in my ear, "Don't you want to get into something, Will?"

Every eye was on me, and suddenly I regretted coming here. Tabitha was old, but reliable news, and at the moment, I found her fucking repulsive. She wiggled and draped herself against me like she owned me. I pulled one arm away, propping my elbow on the table and let the other rest on her lap while I surveyed the scene.

"I'm surprised you've been let out to play tonight," she purred.

I stiffened. "What's your point?"

"Folks are saying Vicky dumped you because you were getting friendly with Red. Don't understand why you'd go from a sure thing to a *no* thing."

My teeth clenched, and my knees instinctively spread. It was only her grip around my neck that kept me from dumping her ass on the ground.

"Guess that brings me right back to a sure thing, don't it, Tabitha?"

The look she gave me should have dropped me dead, but she didn't get out of my lap. I raised my other arm from her and rested it on the table, so she was teetering on my legs. What the fuck was I doing? Same old chicks and same old shit.

Except for a few random, questioning looks thrown my way, the crowd around us had gone back to their own conversations.

"You gone straight, Steele?" Tabitha's voice was like nails on a chalkboard, and I wondered why I'd ever gone down that road.

"Hey, William, we're headed to the line. You coming?" The question came from deep in the crowd.

I was already getting to my feet. Tabitha stumbled to catch her balance but managed to shove me as I walked away, leaving her flailing. Sliding into the driver's seat of my Shelby, I started the car, pulling it into reverse and pulled out of the parking space before pulling the shifter into drive and gunning the engine. The tires spun on the pavement for a brief second before I let off the gas and eased onto the street. I headed to the county line with my mind on Tabitha and how different she was from Margaret. I saw over and over her leaving the hotel, her walk of shame. Who the fuck was I kidding? The last place I needed to be was at the county line racing my car. My mind was a million miles away.

I shut off the white noise of the radio and took the next left. Twenty minutes later I had my car nose deep to the water, sitting on the hood, and wondering just where the hell I'd gone wrong. I had been playing with fire when I pulled Margaret back into that hotel room. No, from the day I'd met her.

TV had been my intention. The idea of curling up with her, holding her, even for a little while, had been exactly what I'd wanted. Right up until she opened that door and the devil pushed me inside. And then all hell broke loose.

My palms slammed against my face, and I fell back onto the hood of my car, throwing my arm over my forehead. How was I going to handle this? I didn't give a shit about Margaret's father, but she did. I had to do this right. Was I willing to fight for her? Yes. Would Margaret appreciate that fight being with her father? Hell fucking no.

Margaret was everything every other girl I knew wasn't. That's what made her stand out. I didn't *want* her to be like every other girl. Fuck, I could get that anywhere. Tabitha would have been a sure thing. I didn't want *that*, didn't want *her*. I liked that Margaret was bashful. Would I do her, given the chance? Hell yes. But, I knew that wasn't what she wanted, and the thought brought me full circle, right back to the middle of no fucking where.

I sat, staring up at the sky until the moon was hidden by the horizon and the sun was breaking in the east. *I have work today. My father will be expecting me.* I shoved myself off the car and headed home for a shower.

"You get a chance to look over those delivery routes?"

My father was sitting behind his desk. The top was littered with papers, and I dropped the folder on top of the rest. "I remapped six of them to include the new distribution site and the new clients."

It had been boring, tedious work, and it had taken everything I had not to fall asleep sitting at the conference table.

My father eyed the folder, nodding. "That's more than I figured you'd get done."

Sitting down in one of the worn, brown leather chairs across from his desk, I waved my hand like it had been nothing. "Anything else for the day?"

He sat back in his chair, eyeing me over his reading glasses. "No. Nothing pertinent." He was watching me. "Vince get off all right?"

I nodded. His eyes met mine and for a moment I had a sinking feeling he was going to start asking questions. Questions I wasn't prepared to answer. I'd be a fool to think he didn't have at least an idea of what was going on in my life.

"Your mother's been worried about you."

Not a question, but he made his point. Fix this shit. My dad would be content to let me live my own life, but he's a piranha when it comes to my mother, and as I thought about Margaret, for the first time in my life, I understood why. I looked away, dipping my head in a subtle nod. Message received.

I let myself out of his office, ignored his ancient secretary, and took the back corridors to the time clock. I punched my card and poured through the door into the late afternoon sun. I checked my watch. If I hurried, I could catch her before her volunteer work at the hospital.

Chapter 22 - Margaret

I HEARD HIM BEFORE I saw him. The rumble of his car grew louder as he approached, pulling past me to park against the curb. I slowed, wondering if I had the strength for this. But, it was William and I couldn't walk away from him. He climbed out of his car, his determined steps bringing him to me way too quickly. I looked ahead, twisting my red and white pinafore tighter in my hands.

"You doing all right, Marguerite?"

I managed a nod. "It's been a little rough."

A brief silence hung over us before William asked, "Can I take you to the hospital?"

There was nothing I wanted more than to get into that car with him and that was all the prompting it took. William pulled open the passenger side door, and I climbed in. We rode in silence, but there were periods where the tension in the car rose as his gaze shifted to me. I kept my attention directed out the window until we pulled up to Bradford Memorial, stopping just a little past the main entrance. William shut the car off and leaned his body against the door.

"I don't even know who I am anymore," I said, truthfully. My eyes burned with tears. I laid my head against the seat, closed them against the sting, and let the frustration slide down my cheeks.

"I know how you feel. I've been trying to sort all this out in my head, and I can't."

William wrapped his fingers around mine and pulled my arm across the console. "I want to go talk to your dad. Make this right."

I was shaking my head. "It's not the time to make a battle of this, William. He's stressed out. He's tired and embarrassed. I picked a horrible time to act all grown up. Very mature, wasn't it?"

"I think we've both been a little selfish. How's your mom?"

"She's better. They gave her some fluids to rehydrate her and kept her overnight just in case. She came home this morning." I pulled my head from the seat and looked at him, needing to draw strength from the kindness I heard in his voice. The sad smile he offered was a poor resemblance of the carefree, happy-go-lucky William was just yesterday.

"Do you want to stop seeing me, Margaret?"

"No." He studied my face a moment, and I realized just how tired and worn out he looked.

"I'll talk to him, Margaret." William was a little more insistent this time.

"What will you tell him, William? That his daughter isn't a little girl anymore? Don't you think he knows that? My mom is dying, and I'm sure all he wants is things back to the way they used to be."

"That's not going to happen and us trying to sneak around isn't going to work in a town the size of a cereal box."

"I know." I couldn't swallow down the frustration raising my voice. "But, I'm not going to rub it in his face, either."

"What are you going to do?"

I rubbed my palms into my eyes trying to grind out the chaos in my mind. "Talk to him. Try to reason with him. I *am* grown. He doesn't have to like it, William, but he'll have to accept it."

William nodded. "OK. If that's what you want to do."

"It's what I'm going to do. I'm not going to stop seeing you, and I'm not going to try and sneak around that."

Rubbing the pad of his thumb across the edge of my nail, William glanced to the entrance of the hospital. "Would you rather go for a ride? Go sit out by the lake, see if we can see the footprints on the moon?"

A hint of a smile was playing on his lips, but I could tell he was exhausted. I shook my head. "I'm already late, and they're expecting me. Besides, I don't think Mr. Armstrong's feet are that big."

William grinned. "Can I at least pick you up and take you home?"

I studied his face, the lack of good color, the way his particular shade emphasized the purple creases under his eyes. "Have you been to bed at all?"

Avoiding me, he turned his eyes toward the windshield, looking out over the grassy area of the hospital's front lawn. "I've had a lot on my mind."

I closed my free hand over his. "How about you sleep tonight and pick me up tomorrow after work?"

William cut his eyes back to me. "Negotiating again?"

I leaned over the console, brushed a kiss across his lips, and pulled myself back into my seat. "It's not negotiable."

I waited for my father to get home from his double shift. He took one look at me sitting at the kitchen table and turned away, shaking his head.

"We can't ignore this," I called after him. "I'm not going to stop seeing William, Daddy."

He stopped but didn't turn around. I could see his head list forward in defeat. The man was exhausted, and I felt horrible for throwing this at him, but I wasn't going to give up William. Period.

"You're going to have to trust me."

Slowly he turned back to me. "Trust you to do the right thing? Trust you to keep an eye on your mother so I can work? Trust you not to get pregnant by some delinquent that's probably got seven kids toddling around town and who's probably having sex with eight other girls? Is that what you want of your life, Margaret?"

I was shaking my head, silent tears sliding down my cheeks. My mom was my world. Taking care of her wasn't an issue for me. I just needed to breathe once in a while. And William wasn't like that. He wasn't like this whole stupid town thought he was. "No, Daddy, and that's not how William is."

"You were in a hotel room with the boy, Margaret."

"Daddy, we could have sex anywhere, it doesn't have to be a hotel room."

His face went red, and his lips disappeared into a thin line as he sucked in his reply. His shoulders raised in a shrug, his hands went out, palms up in frustration. "Don't you think we have enough to deal with in this house? This is not a conversation I want to be having with you, Margaret."

"Then I guess there's nothing more to say."

His gaze went to the floor, and a silence lingered between us. I guess he couldn't find the strength to argue because he turned again, forgetting whatever had brought him to the kitchen in the first place, and made his way upstairs.

As time sped by, the talk of William racing his car faded, along with the gossip about William chasing other girls. By all accounts, he was true to his word.

Mom had handled meeting him as graciously as she could. I don't think Dad ever told her about me sneaking off in the night with William or where he'd found me when she'd gotten sick. If he did, she never brought it up. He didn't either. Dad didn't bring up much of anything after that. He was silent, withdrawn and went out of his way to avoid me. It was heartbreaking, and every time I left the house, I felt like I'd chosen William over my father.

If he could only see the man I was getting to know he'd see William in a whole different light. Instead, he looked at me like I was pushing the boundaries of his limited patience and he just didn't have the energy to adjust to his daughter being an adult.

William focused on his father's business, arguing at the idea of nepotism. His father, Robert, was making him work in all areas of the company, learning it from the bottom up, and William had taken on the challenge with an excitement that made me proud.

My mother seemed to be holding her own, and though she didn't seem to be getting better, she wasn't getting worse. William seemed genuinely distressed the first time he actually met her. "What about treatment?"

I reminded him of our conversation at the park. "She's not choosing to ignore treatment, William. It's not available. There's a difference."

We crossed a street, continuing our walk. People smiled and waved from their porches, but I was sure most of them were shaking their heads after we'd passed.

"What if there was a doctor willing to do it? They make machines to have dialysis done at home. I looked."

The possibility offered too much hope and not enough reality. I eyed William. "We've tried to go that route, William. I appreciate your trying to help, but we just haven't been able to convince anyone to take it on."

He let the conversation go, and I was grateful, but there was another difficult subject I wanted to address with William.

"What do you think President Nixon is going to do about the war? I keep hearing he isn't satisfied with the number of troops. He's talking about drafting men."

"I'm sure he has something in the works. I think he'll do what he can to make it fair," he said.

His answer did nothing to placate me. "What about you?"

"What about me?"

Turning my head toward him, I pulled him to a stop. "Will you go?"

"Yes, if I have to."

The lack of hesitation in his answer crushed me. "Can't you get out of it?"

He pulled me into him. "I can tell you there isn't a person on a draft board that'd be willing to give me a pass. I won't be getting out of it. How could I?"

Frankly, I was surprised he wasn't already enlisted, but the idea that William wouldn't seek a deferment brought some uneasiness to my stomach. "You're an only son." I wrapped my arms around his waist. He held me close, and I knew there was nowhere on Earth I'd ever feel more alive than in his arms.

"The only son situation isn't that cut and dry, and it won't apply to me. There won't be a deferment."

I laid my head on his chest, feeling the weight of his words. "William?"

He grunted a response that reverberated against my cheek. "Kiss me."

I felt him pull his head away, but I hugged him tighter, caught between wanting to stay wrapped in his arms and breaking the moment for the kiss I wanted.

"Right now? Right here on the street? The ladies will swear you've been corrupted, Marguerite."

I loved when he rolled my name off with his ridiculous accent. I pulled away and gave him a playful swat that I was sure did nothing to injure the glorious muscles that rippled under his tight t-shirt. "Let them squeal, I say."

William closed the slight gap between us, bending his head to mine. My lips parted in anticipation just before his tongue grazed them, sending a jolt of electricity through me. I gasped at the effect and William groaned, just before pressing our lips together with an urgency I was learning to understand. Moments later, my hands tangled in his hair, and I became lost in the man until he pulled away, leaving me breathless and confused. I swallowed down the emotion rising in me. My mind was screaming for more.

"I have to admit, I've never been kissed quite like you kiss me before," I breathed.

"Took you long enough to answer the question, Marguerite." He was being playful, but he seemed to be struggling in his own right. "We can't be doing too much of that," he said.

The nightmare from the hotel was at the forefront in both our minds, but the feel of William's lips pressed against mine always made me want more. "I feel…I don't even know how I feel," I said. "Let's do it again?"

With a cocky grin, William obliged, hungrier, harsher, but yet my body responded in kind instead of retreating. His large hand went to my face, sliding down to cup my neck, pulling me against him. As if I'd run away. I was incapable. I was helpless. I was in love with William Steele. When he pulled away, I felt like the oxygen had been sucked from the atmosphere.

"Fuck, Margaret." He rested his forehead against mine, a frustrated release of his warm breath brushing my face.

"Is it like this with all the other girls?"

William folded me into his arms.

"You mean has a simple kiss always made me want to fuck someone so bad? No."

I shouldn't have been flattered by the words. But, I was. Something new and exciting settled in the pit of my stomach, and I held William a little tighter.

"Your language is atrocious, William."

He laughed. "Come on, let's walk it off."

We headed in the direction of the park and went to the swings. With school back in session, it was empty, and dusk had chased away the daylight, so there was an aura of privacy there. William sat on the swing and guided me to him. "Sit in my lap."

"I'm in a dress," I whispered, looking around at the empty park.

"I know," William said, laughing. "You're always in a dress."

Heat raced through my body. I may have been inexperienced, but I had been privy to the locker room gossip about what the boys did to girls, even vice versa. My body tingled at the thought, and then I caught William's eye. I was drawn to him. I wanted him to touch me. God help me, I hoped there'd be time to pray for redemption because I couldn't tell him no.

I settled into his lap as demurely as I could. "Hold on to the chains," he instructed.

Doing as I was told, I wrapped each hand around the warm metal and let my eyes fall shut. Just the anticipation of what he could do to me had me feeling dizzy with emotions. His hands landed on my legs and slid up, slowly exposing my thighs to the cool night air. "I just want to touch you."

His raspy voice sent a wave of warm breath against my cheek. Rough hands glided against my skin until they were under my skirt, tracing the edging of my panties. The warmth of his hands against my cool skin sent a shiver through my body.

His fingers trailed the lace and came together over my belly. The tender touch traveled up past my navel, his fingers separating again as his hands traced my ribs and flattened against my sides. My elbows closed in, trapping his hands against me.

His lips brushed my cheek, and I instinctively turned my head toward him, seeking more. Locked in a kiss, William's hands slipped from my hold, skimming along my arms. Releasing me from the kiss, William locked his fingers around my wrists.

"I have never wanted anyone as much as I want you right now."

A long breath floated through my hair as his hands drifted down, spreading my dress back over my knees. "Or been more willing to wait."

His forehead landed on the back of my hair, and I leaned into him, every inch of my body aching to have his hands back on me. William wrapped his arms around me, pulling me into him.

"I don't want you to stop." My breathless words brought a quiet sigh from William. "Touch me. Please."

He planted a kiss in my hair and patted my side like I should get up.

"Not out here, Margaret."

Disappointed, I stood, straightening my dress. William took my hand in his and led me back toward my house. "Do you mind asking your parents if you can go out for a bit?"

I looked at him, curious, but went inside to ask while he waited by the car. My father would do no more than shrug and shake his head, knowing I would go anyway. When I came back with a jacket, he took my hand again and led me to the driver's side, opening the door. "You drive."

My mouth open fell in surprise. William was particular about his car, but I couldn't resist sliding into the seat. I grinned, watching him stride around the front of the car and climb in beside me.

"Are you sure about this?" I asked.

He nodded and handed me the keys. After making some adjustments with the seat and mirrors, I started the engine. "Where are we going?"

"Go straight, and take a right on Shepard Street."

Pulling the shifter into drive, I checked for traffic and eased the car onto the road. Every inch of me was tense, wondering if this was a mistake. There was no way I could pay if I damaged his car. I risked a glance at William, who was staring straight ahead, at ease having me in control of his pride and joy.

Rolling to a stop at a stop sign, I turned to him. "Are we going racing?" I was smiling, joking, in spite of my nerves.

"That what you want to do?"

"Ha, not hardly." I made the turn and concentrated on my driving. William continued to give me directions until I realized we were going to his house. I pulled into a gravel drive that split a grove of oak trees with a knot in my stomach.

"Pull around to the side of the house."

I followed William's instructions, trying to keep my attention from getting pulled away by the stately home growing bigger with our approach.

"I wish you'd warned me I was meeting your parents."

He was already out, coming for me. He opened my door, refusing to give me a chance to protest. "They're not here."

I froze, and William tugged me toward him. "You won't have to tell me, Margaret. No sex. But, I'm not going to fondle you in the park like a whore."

A nervous giggle erupted from me as I fell into step beside him. We raced up the steps, and William let us in, pushing the door shut behind us.

"You want something to drink?"

Shaking my head, I took in what little I could of the surroundings. It was getting dark, and the mass of trees shaded the house so well, there was very little natural light. We were in a foyer with a hall directly in front of us and a huge open living area to our left. To the right was a massive staircase. William led me upstairs, keeping my hand in his past two doors to his room.

It was clean; tidy, with a large bed dominating the space. Shelves of model cars and books lined the walls, and a nearby dresser was littered with discarded pocket change and pictures.

"Not what I expected," I said.

William grinned. "What did you expect?"

Shrugging, I realized I hadn't really thought about it. I had never pictured myself in his room.

"Where are your parents?"

"Visiting my mother's relatives in Tennessee. They won't be back until Friday."

"How long have they been gone?"

William crossed his arms over his chest. "Four days."

There was hesitation in his voice as if he'd been deliberately avoiding this predicament. I fingered a copy of *A Tale of Two Cities* and pulled it from its shelf, holding it up.

"My mother," William explained.

"Sydney or Charles?"

"Sydney."

The lack of hesitation made me smile. I slid it back in place and finished my inspection of his room while that sank in.

"We can go downstairs and watch TV if you want to, Margaret."

Considering our situation, I was both pleased and disappointed that William hadn't told me they were gone. I made a pass by his door, flicking off the light as I went by and moved to stand in front of him, sidling myself between his knees. "I don't want to go, William. I didn't want to leave the park. I didn't want you to stop touching me."

My face was side by side with his. I could hear his breathing in my ear. I reached for the zipper on my dress and eased it down, closing my eyes and listening as his steady breathing hitched and held. I pulled away and let my dress fall.

Chapter 23 - William

MARGARET IN MY ROOM wasn't a good idea. I couldn't breathe. The sight of her revealing herself to me, knowing my limitations…it was a goddamn minefield. I froze. How the hell was I going to do this, put on the brakes and keep my promise? What the fuck was I thinking, bringing her here?

"William?"

Her soft hands hugged my face, tilting me up to her. It was too dark to see any emotion in her eyes, and when I hesitated, Margaret took the reins, leaning her body into mine, kissing me. My resolve broke. I wrapped my arms around her, laying back on the bed and pulling her on top of me, never breaking our kiss.

My hands found the hook to her bra, and I released the clasp. Rolling her over, I settled my body beside her, running my fingers over her skin, burying my face in her hair, soaking up the smell of her.

Her tiny hand drifted up my arm, under the sleeve of my shirt. I paused, yanking it off and throwing it away. I needed my skin against hers. By her side again, Margaret's hands roamed my back, my sides. Christ, it was like she was starving for me, and I was throbbing with a need to sustain that.

Sliding my hands under the lace of her bra, my hand cupped her and squeezed. I captured Margaret's moan with another kiss and tugged the material away so that my fingertips could glide freely over her.

Margaret squirmed, and I broke our kiss to move farther down her body, swirling my tongue around her pebbled nipple, rolling the other between my fingers. Margaret wrapped her arms around my neck, pulling me closer to her, her soft gasps and the unfamiliar feeling seeming to overwhelm her for a moment. When she relaxed, I moved my hand down her belly, over her underwear, and between her legs. I groaned, and Margaret whimpered. She was so fucking wet.

So much for taking my damn time. I couldn't wait to touch her. I slid my hand past the elastic of her panties and into her warmth.

I laid my head beside hers. "Open your legs," I whispered.

She did, and I slid my fingers along her, cupping her in my hand. "You ought to feel how wet you are, Margaret."

"I want to touch you."

Bad idea. Very bad idea. I moved my fingers up to circle her clit, trying to pay attention to her response and not the fact that I was about to cum in my pants. Margaret gasped, her hand flying out to cover mine.

"Relax." I kissed her cheek. "Relax, Margaret."

Her body twitched, and Margaret muttered my name. It was her gateway. Her body relaxed, and her hips rolled against my touch.

"That feels good, don't it?"

Without an answer, Margaret shifted toward me, bringing my lips to hers. "I want to touch you."

She was tugging at my jeans again, but there was no way I was stopping to take my pants off.

"William."

A ripple of pure lust slammed through me with her plea. "You first."

Ignoring me, Margaret blindly fumbled with my jeans. She managed to pull the button free, but stilled when I shifted my touch to a firmer stroke.

Her body locked in my arms. "Oh God."

My stomach tensed, knowing she was close. My hips rocked against her hand, and she pressed her palm against my straining erection.

Fuck me.

Moments later, Margaret was grabbing my arms, gripping her thighs around my hand. Her body convulsed with release, sending an unexpected shudder through me. Her sensuous cry filled the room, and I groaned in frustration at my own need.

Margaret's body stiffened as she found her peak and her desperate cry of my name faded off into a moan as her body began to recover.

Still cupping her, I flattened my palm to rub her desire back onto her skin. "I'm sure that's about the hottest fucking thing I've ever done," I panted, still rubbing her. She leaned in to kiss me softly, her hand finding my zipper and sliding it down.

My eyes fell shut, waiting for her soft hand to wrap around me. The first unsure touch sent a jolt of electricity through my body. I jerked at the feel and wrapped my arms around her, needing to anchor myself to her.

It wasn't the most skilled handjob I'd ever had, but if I thought bringing Margaret to orgasm was hot, holding her in my arms while she stroked me kicked things up a thousand degrees.

I could feel those beautiful green eyes watching me, and it intensified every second. Her tiny fingers tightened, and my hips rolled, sending her grip gliding to the base of my cock and back to the tip.

"Like that?"

Her hand had already caught the rhythm, and I could feel the tension in my stomach winding taut for my own release, fueled by her lusty question. I could only imagine what it would feel like to bury myself in her.

It was my undoing. The strain in my groin exploded, sending wave after wave of heat and pleasure through me until I couldn't contain it. I buried my face in Margaret's neck to stifle the eruption of profanity that came with it.

Holy fuck. I sucked in a breath. "Margaret," I whimpered, speechless. Never had it been like this. My entire body was sapped of energy, aching, but I'd never felt more alive.

"I want to do it again," she purred.

I laughed at her enthusiasm, pulling air into my lungs. "Another time." Damn, there were so many things I wanted to do to this girl. She was glowing, her eyes bright and shining with our secret. I leaned in, planting a soft kiss on her lips. "I can't take you home smelling like sex."

"But we didn't have sex," she said, but she was grinning with mischievousness.

I pulled my hand to cup her face. "No, but your dad will know we did something," I warned her with a grin.

A hint of regret flashed in her eyes.

"Don't, Margaret. Don't regret this." I pulled her to me, kissing her cheek, her nose, and then her lips before I rolled her to her back, crushing her tiny frame between the bed and me. "It's just us. No one will know."

Face to face, skin to skin felt like the most natural thing in the world to me. My heart wouldn't accept regret. Not from her.

My thumb brushed away an errant tear, and I rested my forehead against hers. The words were right there on the tip of my tongue, but I wasn't sorry for what we'd done. I swallowed the apology.

"You probably think I'm crazy," she whispered, her voice thick with emotion.

I thought for a moment, putting myself in her position, weighing everything she'd just done against everything she believed in. The answer was obvious. You could feel it in the room, in her touch, her words. She loved me.

I drew up my knees, forcing her legs up and around me, needing to get closer to her. I slid my arms beneath her shoulders and cradled her head in my hands, raising her ear to my lips. "I don't think you're crazy, Margaret," I whispered back. "I know how you feel about me. I can feel it. It seeps from you like a scent."

Her wet cheek pressed to mine, and her arms tightened around me. "Kiss me, William."

Now how could I resist that?

Chapter 24 - Margaret

THE FEEL OF WILLIAM'S body pressed against mine was heavenly, and that was the problem. Was there no road I wouldn't follow this man down, nothing I would deny him?

No, because denying him would mean denying myself what I secretly wanted: his lips on mine, his hands on me, quieting those desires screaming out in my mind for attention. I wanted him. I wanted all of him and not just for today. I wanted him forever.

His kiss, tender and sweet, conveyed everything my mind needed to hear. This wasn't a love come lately. This was a together forever kind of life-sustaining force, and I was powerless.

William paused in his kiss. "You OK?"

I nodded, feeling his fingers on the back of my head.

"We should get cleaned up."

Despite his words, William didn't move, and neither did I. Every inch of skin in contact with his was hypersensitive, connected with need, sweat and the promise of more. "I don't want to go just yet," I breathed.

There was a subtle tensing of William's muscles as if he was reading my mind, and I felt myself flush in the darkness. We'd never have this moment again, and I wasn't ready to let it go.

"OK."

His voice was edged with stress and desire and that made me bold and reckless. "I want you." My nails scraped down his back to the waist of the jeans he still wore, sliding inside and pulling him against me.

"Margaret, don't do this, we'll wait."

I dipped my hips into the mattress, pulling him tighter against me. "I *have* waited. Waited for the right one."

Despite William's protests, his body overruled, and I felt him harden against the wet underwear I still wore.

"Fuck, Margaret."

A throaty groan rose from me. "Your language is atrocious, William. Now take these off," I said, tugging at his pants again.

With a knowing sigh, William stood, shedding the rest of his clothes. Naked, he reached for my underwear, and I raised my hips so that he could pull them off. Tossing them to the floor, William reached for my thighs and pulled me to the edge of the bed. He sat me up, wrapping his arms around me and pulling me to his chest. I rested a moment, feeling the pounding of his heart against my cheek, taking in the scent of combined pleasure. This was it. This is where I was meant to be.

William's fingers fisted my hair and gently tugged my face up to his. From somewhere down the hall, a light burned, creating enough glow in his room to illuminate his face, and I blinked at the fierceness of what I saw in his eyes. His lips crashed over mine, claiming me, uniting us.

We were both breathless when he released me. I found myself on my back again, our short, labored breaths echoing in the room. Seeking permission or doubt one final time, William gave a subtle nod at what he saw in my eyes and dipped his head to capture my nipple with his teeth.

There was a tangible difference in the air as William drove me home, my hand in his, his grip firmer yet more relaxed than before. Neither of us spoke. In fact, very little had been said in the last few hours, yet so much had changed. There was hardly a part of me that William's lips, fingers, and tongue hadn't discovered, yet he stopped short of making love to me, and I was both satiated and disappointed. Happy and confused. I sighed at the overwhelming emotions.

As if reading my thoughts, William pulled my hand to his lips and kissed my fingers, settling my hand on his thigh and covering it with his own. I studied him in the random light of oncoming cars, intermittent street lights. He'd gotten his hair cut short, a little longer on top than on the sides, but it suited him. His profile was more distinct without the distraction of the mass of curls. He'd lost some of his boyish style, and the effect only made him more appealing.

I dropped my gaze with another sigh. How could it be wrong to feel so strongly about anyone? Not anyone, someone, him. *William Steele.*

"What?"

My head jerked back to him. Did I say his name out loud? "What do you mean what?"

William steered the car to the curb and none-to-gently hit the brakes. He shoved the shifter into park and turned off the engine, his attention focused on something off in the distance.

"I can see it on your face, Margaret. Do you remember?" he asked. "At the diner, you said you weren't sure if my ego could handle the rejection?"

He wasn't looking at me, but I nodded my response, afraid to trust my voice. I pulled my hand away from his thigh, suddenly aware that his touch was gone.

He put his elbow on the door and rubbed his fingers across his forehead. "It has never been about me, Margaret. Not when it comes to you. Do you know what I'd do for you?"

His gaze turned to me, and my heart froze.

"Anything." He studied me a moment before turning away, rubbing the emotion from his eyes with the palms of his hands. "Everything I do, every choice I make, I think, 'How will Margaret feel about this?' I know everything I do in this fucking town comes back to you, and *that* is what matters to my ego." His voice lowered. "My dad would call it growing up, being responsible, being a man. My mom would call it being in love."

Tears were streaming down my face. I couldn't put a coherent thought together before William reached across the console, pulling me to him, pressing his lips to mine, and cupping my face in his hands. There was no hunger, no breach of his tongue, just his lips sealing the moment with mine.

There was a firm tap on the window, and William and I jumped apart, noticing for the first time the glow of blue lights fading in and out of the car. William rolled down the window, and the officer peered inside, glancing at William, and then focusing his attention on me.

"Are you all right?"

"We were just sitting here," William protested, his palms up on the defensive.

I touched his arm, assuring the officer I was fine. "He was just taking me home."

The officer glanced back to William, not bothering to hide the dubious look on his face.

"Do you want my license?" William asked.

"Don't need 'em," the officer smirked.

"Then can we go?" William's irritation was obvious, but it didn't rattle the officer. He looked back to me.

"To take you home, yes."

He stepped back, giving William just enough room to pull the car onto the street. He did, glancing in the rearview mirror as he pulled away shaking his head, but he said nothing.

I, on the other hand, was in a whirlwind. I glanced at William, taking in his white-knuckled grip on the steering wheel, the muscle clenching and releasing in his jaw.

Headlights fell in behind us, and I could tell from William's demeanor that the officer wasn't ready to put his faith in William as I had. Impulsively, I leaned across, kissing William's ear. "Screw him."

Chapter 25 - William

I COULDN'T HELP BUT laugh. My little renegade. I just never knew what to expect out of her.

"Can I ask you something?"

"Sure," I said.

"Would you mind taking me to see *Easy Rider* next weekend?"

I eyed her for a moment before bringing my attention back to the road, not knowing why it surprised me. I had seen the movie with buddies already, but if Margaret wanted to see it, I could do it again.

"I can do that."

I pulled up to her house, shutting off the car and as expected, the patrolman cruised by, watching us. I shook my head, turning back to Margaret. They irritated me, but I was used to the fuckers. "Are you OK?"

"You can't be serious, William."

Rubbing a nervous hand through my still damp hair, I stared at her knowing I'd find no hint of lying in her eyes, but I needed reassurance, and this was something I wasn't used to.

I smiled and got out, opening her door and walking her to the gate. She came in close, her body brushing against mine and filling the air with the fresh scent of soap. She swayed in her effort to stand on her tip toes and look me in the eye. "I said I wanted to do it again," she said, quietly. "And I'm sure there's a lot more than that waiting for me," she added with a grin.

This girl was full of surprises. All I could do was smile as she planted a last kiss on my lips and breezed through the gate. She turned back to me and in a whisper added, "Next time, I get to do some exploring."

She left me standing there, mouth open in surprise, a new and steady ache in my groin at the promise.

I watched her disappear into the house and waited for the light to come on in her room. I didn't want to leave, but I expected any minute that pig would come back by to make sure I was out of here. With a last look, I climbed back into my Shelby and headed straight for home.

Back in my room, I stripped and climbed in bed, but the scent of Margaret was strong and fresh, and so were the memories of tonight. Never in my life had I turned a chick down. Not one that I wanted, anyway. But then again, Margaret was no *chick*. She was different. She was a woman. And she was *mine*.

I rolled over, gathering the blankets under my chin. I'd never gone down on a girl until tonight, had never wanted to. The idea had never appealed to me until I started kissing on Margaret. Every touch, every kiss brought a reaction from her that took me to a whole other level. I didn't want to just have sex with her. I wanted to draw out those sighs. I wanted to hear her moan my name over and over.

Margaret kicked things up a notch, and it wasn't just because we weren't going *that* far. It was because of how I felt about her, how she made me feel about myself.

Flipping over, restless, I considered introducing her to my parents. I'd never done that before, and the thought brought a smile to my face. Wouldn't my mother be shocked at the wholesome young lady who'd stolen her son's heart?

Chapter 26 - Margaret

WILLIAM AND I HAD been seeing each other for almost two months, and Saturday was our first opportunity to get out of town and enjoy one another's company. It was, in the grand scheme of things, the first *real* date we'd had. One where we weren't confined by the limits of our small town or the fact that William's ex-girlfriend's parents owned the only real eating establishment around.

He picked me up early, insisting on taking me out to a proper dinner. There was a steakhouse close by the drive-in where *Easy Rider* was playing, and we would go there first. He opened the passenger door of the Shelby and closed it behind me. This was exciting, and I settled in to enjoy my night as he climbed in the driver's seat and started the car.

"Have you heard from Tammy?"

"Yes, they're settled in. She's already complaining about school, but she'll hang in there."

"I haven't heard anything from Vince."

"Tammy said he's working at a garage outside of town. They're amazed by him, according to her."

William dipped his head. "He's a smart dude."

Dialing in the radio, he brought the station in clearer, turned up the volume and rested his hand on my thigh as he drove. A comfortable silence fell in between the intermittent songs we'd sing along with on the radio, and it seemed in no time at all, the winding country roads and sporadic buildings gave way to a busier highway and bigger, more congested cropping of businesses.

We pulled into the parking lot of the two-story log cabin turned restaurant and went inside. After just a few minutes of waiting for our table, we took our seats and shared a smile.

"I'm curious," William said. "What makes you want to see *Easy Rider*?"

I eyed the rustic décor of the restaurant, avoiding William's gaze. "Mostly because I think it's brave of them to take off across the country on motorcycles. I've heard about the ending." My voice trailed off, grasping at something I couldn't understand.

"You'll like it," he said.

A waitress came and took our orders. William filled the time we waited for our food filling me in on his latest work at Steele, Inc. He was learning everything he could and was making notes in each department he worked in with ideas to streamline efficiency and improve things, even the environment for the workers.

"Dad seems open to my ideas."

"He ought to be," I said, leaning back to make room for the waitress to set our food on the table. "It's probably been a long time since he's spent any significant amount of time in the departments you're working in. He's busy, but new ideas never hurt."

We ate, lingering over our food as our conversation dragged out.

"I also talked to Dad about your mom. Well, not *your* mom, specifically, but renal disease in general. He's done some digging on the treatment and dialysis. There's rumor your dad's constant letters may have reached someone. I don't know who, but the idea is to make dialysis covered by Medicare so that more people who needs it can get it."

William dug into his pocket and slid a piece of paper across the table. "This doctor will be getting in touch with your mom. He sees a future in clinics where they do nothing but dialysis, especially if this bill goes through, but he doesn't want to wait until then to get involved. He's setting up a foundation to do some in home dialysis. The goal is to collect treatment data and use it to lobby for support for this Medicare bill. That'll take some time, but he's a specialist, and he's willing to take on treatment until then."

My mind was racing with the information William was feeding me. "Treatment? My mom will get dialysis?"

William nodded. "And no committee because it's all going to be privately funded. No expenses for the patients. Dr. Moore will be making all the decisions himself."

I sat back against the chair trying to sort out exactly what all this meant, afraid to get my hopes up and even more afraid I wouldn't be able to stop them from soaring.

"How do you know he'll accept my mom?" I asked, feeling a little suspicious.

William winked and smiled. "I just know."

I didn't care how. All I knew was that my mother would be getting treatment, and I had the man in front of me to thank for it. Whatever path he'd taken to get us to this point, I didn't care, but it was obvious he hadn't had to go to jail to get it done.

"I love you, William." The words seeped out of my conscience and formed into words before I could think. "Not just for this, for my mom, but because I…I just love who you are and what we are together."

"Feels pretty powerful, don't it?"

I nodded at his description.

"Rare?"

I continued my slow nod.

"Unbreakable?"

Yes. Yes, all of those things. A single tear slid down my cheek as my heart accepted that William had given meaning to the emotions I'd been feeling. He could only describe them so perfectly if he felt them, too.

He smiled knowingly and slid from his seat. He put money on the table to cover the check that hadn't yet come and pulled me from my seat, holding my hand as we crossed the rustic dining room and went outside. At the car, William cupped his hand against my face and leaned in for a soft kiss. "Let's go see a movie."

He let me in and walked around to the driver's side. "There'll be a line of cars waiting to get in. We need a good spot," he said, starting the car.

Minutes later we were pulling onto the dirt path that would lead us to the ticket booth. William was right. Already there were eight or nine cars waiting to pay and be let into the drive-in to park. He shoved the car in park and switched off the engine, angling in his seat so his body faced me and eyed me curiously.

Chapter 27 - William

"HAVE YOU BEEN TO a drive-in before?"

I watched her squirm in her seat, keeping her eyes on the car parked in front of us.

"No."

"You'll like it," I said with a grin.

"My parents aren't much on this sort of thing."

"Movies or drive-ins?"

She shot me a look, and I couldn't help but laugh. "You didn't tell them where we were going, did you?"

Margaret raised her chin. "I told them we were going to the movies."

Maybe it was the wistful look on her face; maybe it was that my mind read its own meaning into her words. My cock twitched at the unspoken thoughts that lingered between us. I'd be lying if I said I hadn't played a hundred different scenarios of how tonight would go.

Shaking my head, I leaned across the console, sliding my hand up her thigh as I did, stopping just short of the juncture to her groin. "Are you needing me to get you off again, Margaret?"

My fingertips danced lightly over her skin, and her head fell back against the seat, but her green eyes remained fixed on me.

"I told you I wanted to do it again."

If she didn't have my attention before, the way she breathed those words created an instant shortage of space in my jeans. "You dirty little girl. You planned this!"

A hint of a smile played on her lips, but there was no shame in the brazen look she sent my way. Her eyes were alight with desire. Need. A need for me. She leaned across and pressed her lips to mine, telling me everything I needed to know as she shared her soul with me. I drank it up until horns sounded behind us, and we were forced to pull apart. Keeping my eyes on her, I started the car and pulled the shifter into drive, waiting to turn my head forward until the car began to drift ahead, bringing us up to the ticket booth.

I pulled my wallet from my jeans, passed the cash to the attendant, and followed the line of cars around the fence to the parking area. Without giving it any thought, I pulled the Shelby into the last parking spot on the last row, giving us as much privacy as the drive-in would allow.

"Let's go get some snacks."

Margaret nodded at my suggestion and climbed out of the car, taking my hand as we made our way to the concession building. It sat, centered in the middle of the parking area, built low to the ground to keep from obstructing the view of those parked behind it. Inside, railings formed a zig-zag path that kept customers moving, and it was there we waited, me standing behind Margaret, her back resting against my front. From my stance behind her, I had a nice aerial view of her cleavage.

Her body trembled in my arms, and I realized she was trying not to laugh.

"What?" I bent down so that only she could hear me, though eavesdropping was unlikely in the noisy building with poor acoustics.

She turned her face toward me to be sure she was heard. "I can feel you staring at me. I bet you want to touch me."

Her words reached around me like a vise, but I could tell by the color creeping up her neck, she wasn't unaffected by my adoration of her tits. "I bet you want me to."

We edge further up the line, and she nodded her head in answer to my statement. I squeezed her against me in what would seem like an innocent hug to those surrounding us, but it would tell Margaret exactly how her sexy playfulness was affecting me.

"You always this horny?" she whispered.

I feigned shock. "This is your fault, woman. You do this; you make me this way. And apparently, you do it on purpose."

By the time we reached the counter, I was in the midst of another full blown erection. Christ, you would think I was a twelve-year-old peeping in the girl's locker room. I could only hope the waist-high counter was high enough to keep it hidden. We placed our orders and moved along the line, collecting our snacks as we went. Margaret grabbed our drinks at the end of the line and turned to me.

"I should use the bathroom before we go back to the car." We walked to one of the few tables in the building and she sat the drinks down. "I'll be back in a minute."

I slid into a seat, waiting and thinking. Margaret radiated everything that was right in my world. I'd have a lifetime to lose myself in her, but it wouldn't start tonight. Margaret may have wavered when things had gotten hot and heavy, but I knew on some level she'd regret it, and I didn't want to be a part of that. She'd said she wanted to wait. As much as I wanted to bury my cock inside of her, I was just as adamant about her having that moment.

Flashbacks of our evening at my house played through my mind, but my resolve was settled. Everything up to penetration was fair game, and my thoughts were already on the near future.

Chapter 28 - Margaret

DUSK HAD FALLEN BY the time we left the concession building. I wasn't all that surprised that William followed me to the passenger seat, sliding in and pushing the seat back as far as it would go. He patted his lap, indicating I should slide into the seat with him.

Handing him the drinks, I waited until he was settled to crawl into his lap. He adjusted our seating, crooking his arm to offer some padding between me and the door.

In front of us, the enormous white screen flickered to life with the animated dancing of hot dogs and snacks. We ate our snacks in silence, watching the screen, previews of movies to come, and the introduction to *Easy Rider*. I wasn't very hungry after that huge dinner, but I was suddenly shy about my intentions for the night.

"I should have at least hung the speaker in the window," William said.

There was a palpable tension between us, a sexual conversation leading us down a path I longed for us to go, but was unsure how to start. Finally, I turned and caught his lips with mine, stroking his face with my fingers as he returned the kiss.

"Don't bother," I said.

He resumed our kiss, and my fingers drifted down his face, his neck, reaching the buttons on his shirt and freeing them as I went. When I reached the point where his shirt disappeared into his jeans, I pushed my hand inside the open fabric and ran my hand over him, exploring the dips and valleys of his muscular stomach before my fingertips drifted over his nipple.

He groaned softly, and I continued to stroke my fingertips over the area, trading tactics on occasion and running my fingernails over him.

Following my lead, William unzipped my cotton dress with the front zipper, pulled the fabric over my breast, and flicked his tongue over my hardened nipple.

For the first time, I glanced around us, taking in how precarious our privacy really was. There was a gap of three or four spaces between us and the closest car… I couldn't really tell in the dark. It was shrouded in darkness, too, much like William's Shelby, with the only real light reaching any of us being the reflection of the big screen. On the other side of us there was just woods.

William sensed my anxiety and pulled away.

"Can we get in the back?" I asked.

He leaned across and pulled the lever that unlocked the back of the driver's seat. He pushed it forward and sat back, making room for me to climb through the space. Clumsily, I did, waiting while he pushed the seat back, scooted to the driver's window, and brought the speaker in. He turned it almost all the way down, hung it on the window, and rolled it back up as far as it would go with the speaker in place. He pulled the passenger seat forward, leaving it in place when he joined me in the back.

William settled in with his back against the side of the passenger side of the car, throwing his leg over the hump that separated the backseats. He pulled me onto his lap. "That better?"

I wanted to answer, but the wanton woman in me was already flinging myself against William, seeking out his touch, needing his hands to erase the chill that had set in since his warm hands had left me. He reclined as best he could in the confines of the car and pulled me against him, pulling my dress up to my waist as he did.

His hands landed on the back of my upper thighs and gently squeezed before one hand slid over my right cheek and inside my panties. Even as his fingers slid between my legs, his other hand trailed my back and twisted in my hair. He knew exactly where to touch me, and my body trembled with each slow, deliberate pass of his fingers over my delicate skin.

"I can't wait to do this again with my tongue, Margaret." My breath caught, and I clenched around his fingers. His groan reverberated against me. "You like that thought."

I didn't have to admit to it. By now, William knew me like no one else ever had, and the fact that he wanted to do things like that to me brought me that much closer to release.

I pulled away, wanting to delay the inevitable. I pushed open the folds of William's shirt and began mimicking and kissing his chest, teasing my tongue over his nipples the way he did mine. As I did, my hand slid to his jeans and with a gentle tug, the button was free, and I pushed the zipper down. William raised his hips and tugged them down. With my small frame moving easy in the confined space of the car, I moved down his belly, trailing a path with my tongue and teeth to his erection.

"Margaret?"

I ignored the questioning tone as he called my name and instead drew a wet line down his length with my tongue.

"Fuck, Margaret."

I had no idea what I was doing, but I took my cues from William, concentrating on him as I explored his body. Nothing I did seemed to displease him, and he seemed content to let me experiment as I saw fit. That is, until I closed my mouth over him, and he grabbed himself, squeezing and panting, "Stop, Margaret, Jesus fucking Christ, stop a minute."

My eyes were adjusted enough to the dark, and the movie gave just enough light that when I pulled away, I could watch the rapid rise and fall of his belly, the way his head rolled against the side of the car with his eyes closed and his features twisted in intense concentration. It struck me that he was, at that moment, the simplest definition of lust I would ever know.

When his grip relaxed, I resumed my assault. There was nothing the man could ask of me that I would deny him.

His hands slipped inside my open dress and tugged my bra up over my breasts until they hung free. He tweaked and pulled each nipple between his fingers as I sucked on him and the dampness between my legs grew until I could feel the moisture spread to my panties.

"I want to taste you."

I didn't get a chance to think before William had me pulled upright into his lap, me facing him and him now sitting on the hump. He gently laid me back, supporting me with his knees and the console. It was uncomfortable, but all thoughts of that were lost as William ripped the sides of my underwear and pulled them free. He pushed my knees against the seats, opening me up to him.

A coolness rushed over me, stealing my body heat in the second it took William to cover me with his mouth. After that, all reasoning was lost.

Chapter 29 - William

IF THIS DIDN'T WORK, I'd already decided we'd disappear into the woods. The smell of her arousal was already thick in the car. I had to have her, taste her.

As soon as my mouth touched her, Margaret bucked against the feel. I heard her breath catch over the faint sound of the movie and the soft moan of resignation as she gave in to the sensation of my tongue moving over her.

"Oh my God, William, that feels so good."

Each subtle flick of my tongue brought a gasp from her, a sharp intake of breath, a mumbled word. Each whimpered reaction brought me one heartbeat closer to my own orgasm, and it didn't seem to matter that she wasn't touching me. The only stimulation I needed was her responses to my touch, and she was giving them freely.

I paused a moment to adjust my legs to make it more comfortable on my neck. Margaret protested, grasping at my hair and urging me back to my post.

"I want to come, William, please. God, don't stop."

I groaned at the way my body reacted to her plea. My muscles, already taut with need, screamed at the punishing resistance. My desire to snatch her into my lap and feel her surround me was almost overwhelming. *No, no, no.*

Instead, I sealed my lips around her clit and firmly rocked my head from side to side, letting my tongue rake over her with each pass. Her panting filled the car, her grip on my hair tightened, and I groaned into her.

Margaret bucked one last time and then pressed her hips into my legs as she let go, a stream of words escaping from her mouth I'd never heard her utter before, but in the heat of the moment, it seemed perfectly natural—sexy. I found myself struggling to hold back as her words morphed into a frustrated cry as she attempted to both push into and escape the pleasure I was giving her.

I gave in and sat up, bringing Margaret with me. For just a moment I held her warm flesh against me, tangling my hands in her hair and pulling her to me for a kiss. She immediately understood my need and stroked herself against me until I couldn't hold back anymore.

My feet locked against the floor, and I forced Margaret against me, creating the pressure I needed to take me over the edge. Impatient, I grabbed her hips and tilted her against me. Her green eyes disappeared behind closed lids. I knew she was mine for the taking, but that was a gift to await us both.

"I want you inside me. Please."

It wasn't an option, but hearing the words tore away my constraint. For a split second, I was overwhelmed with my surroundings, of Margaret, the feel of her body against me. The next, I was lost in a vortex of confusion, relying on instinct to drive the thrusts needed to take me over the edge.

Margaret whimpered with frustration as I found my release, heightening the moment of another opportunity lost.

Collapsing, Margaret's body lay limp against me, and I was content to hold her there. As our breathing returned to normal and our bodies recovered from the moment, Margaret's body heaved a sigh, and I became worried.

"Are you upset?" I asked, rubbing my chin in her hair.

There was a short pause before she answered. "Why would I be upset?"

My normally filthy mouth now seemed tempered with unease. "Because I didn't…because we didn't…"

Margaret sat up, eyeing me suspiciously. "Have sex?" My mouth fell open, but Margaret laughed and wiggled against me. "It was nice exactly like it was. Thank you."

I didn't have to ask for what. Her desire to wait until her wedding night was made clear from day one. I was secure enough to know that moment would be with me and toeing the line such as we were, I was content to wait.

Chapter 30 - Margaret

IF I NEVER FOUND myself in the arms of another man, I'd die a happy woman. I lay back against his chest, my contentment so strong that my mind had not yet caved to the shame I should be feeling, the shame I knew was coming. It had last time, but that hadn't stopped me from working this out tonight. If my body were, in fact, sacred, surely no one could worship it the way William Steele just had.

I settled in, listening to the faint sounds of the movie from the speaker. The sound of motorcycles filled the car, and William shifted in his seat. "You at least need to see the ending." I refused to budge from my perch against his warm skin, sweaty as it was.

"I know how it ends." Sure enough, a distant gun blast sounds from the speaker followed by the racing of another motorcycle engine. There was some dialogue I couldn't make out, another gunshot, and then an explosion. Moments later music played, and I guessed that ending credits were rolling. I huffed childishly, pouting that our night was over.

"We better go get cleaned up."

I sat up with a groan and zipped my dress. I pulled it down as best I could, but opted to get out on the safe passenger side where I could hide in the shadows and readjust if I needed to.

Once I was out, William pulled his jeans up, buttoned his shirt, and crawled out behind me. Working our way against the traffic leaving the drive-in, William and I made our way to the concession building and our respective bathrooms. I gathered a mass of paper towels and wet them, remembering that my underwear was somewhere in William's car.

I cleaned up as quickly as I could and went to meet William back outside. He took my hand as we walked back to the car, giving me a quick kiss before he released me. He started the engine with a roar and filed in line. He looked to me, grinning. "What?"

"I need to educate you," he said.

"About what?" My spirit crashed at the sudden thought that he was disappointed in tonight. "I'm learning," I said, quietly.

"Not that, woman, about the movie, at least the basics. What if your parents ask?"

"I'll tell them I don't remember."

"What if they ask you to tell them about it?"

"I'll tell them two bikers took off cross country and met a lot of not so friendly people along the way."

We made it out to the street, and William turned right into traffic. He cut his eyes at me. "You're going to get us in trouble."

"My parents aren't going to ask me for a detailed description of the motorcycles, William, and we stay in trouble with them."

He ignored me. "An American flag and flames, Margaret. Peter Fonda, Wyatt, drove the flag one and Dennis Hopper, Billy, drove the one with the flames."

"Hopper, flames. Got it, but it won't matter."

William rolled his eyes and laughed as we came to a stop at a red light. His attention drifted from me to a car that pulled up in the lane next to his. I couldn't see who or what it was, but I could tell from the change in William's demeanor that an unspoken conversation was happening. When he looked to me to see my reaction, the car beside him revved the engine a couple of times.

"Thirty seconds. It'll be over before we reach the next light."

I felt my nerves tingle as the realization of what William was asking washed over me. Still riding high from the events of the night, I leaned forward just enough to see the driver beside us framed in a yellow car. Seeing me looking, he leaned forward, splitting his pointer and middle fingers with his tongue as it wagged from his mouth.

The cross lights turned yellow, indicating that any moment we'd have a green light.

"Margaret?"

William's voice was calm, seductively calm. I eased back into my seat and forced my gaze back to him.

"Burn him up," I said, not bothering to hide my disgust at his lewd behavior.

He grinned. "Such a little renegade." He looked back to the driver. Then, in a perfect sequence of events, William coolly nodded, pulled his hand from mine to grab the shifter, and pulled it into low gear just as the light turned green.

Pressed into my seat from the sudden acceleration, a surge of excitement coursed through me. Tires squealed, and my seat vibrated with the power of the engine. Seconds later, William pushed the shifter into a higher gear, and the tempo of the engine changed to a smooth purr as the Shelby picked up speed. I glanced out William's window, but there was no sign of the other car— we'd passed him. It was already over.

William caught my gaze and winked. The light we were approaching was green, yet William let his foot off the accelerator and let the drag slow us down. A yellow Camaro blew past us, honking his horn.

Less than a minute had passed since the Camaro had approached us at the light, but my body and mind were still responding to the rush. I settled back in my seat, laughing at the magic that had just transpired. I was still laughing when we entered the next intersection.

Chapter 31 - William

THERE WAS SOMETHING LAYING on me. It was too heavy, and it hurt. It hurt to breathe. I twisted, trying to force my eyes open to see what was weighing on me so heavily, but the slightest movement brought excruciating pain to my legs. My arms felt heavy, and a constant pinging created a throbbing echo in my ears.

I blinked back the stinging in my eyes, but they instantly watered, blurring the bursts of light I found myself looking into. Voices were coming closer, yelling, the words lost in the throbbing in my ears.

Someone grabbed me and tugged, and I pulled away, gritting. No, it hurt.

"Get the girl, first."

The words bounced in my head. Were they talking about Margaret?"

Whatever was laying on me was jostled around, and this time I couldn't bite back the groan of pain that shot through me.

"I can't get her. I don't think she's breathing, man."

The stranger's voice was near panic, and his lack of composure brought a sense of urgency to me. I forced my eyes open, letting the water that collected in them help to wash the sting away. Gritting my teeth against the pain, I managed to turn my head enough to look up. Shards of glass were raining down around me. My Shelby was resting on the driver's side.

I squeezed my eyes shut. They burned and glass was stinging my face. I tried to turn my head away from the falling glass, but a streak of pain shot down my back. Fuck. I couldn't stifle the cry.

"I think she's dead."

"Who?" The words stuck in my throat, unheard. I forced my eyes open again, long enough to see that Margaret lay on top of me, her lifeless body draping over me like a human blanket. A sob escaped me as I tried to get a response from her. A growl, wounded, pained, and protective was forced from me as I tried to shimmy myself from beneath the weight of her.

"Let us help. Can you lift her to us?"

The voices came to me from where my windshield used to be. I blinked back the blinding tears, trying to see. *Fuck.* I tried to use the palms of my hands to wipe my vision clear. I blinked. *Fuck.* Nothing was helping. I squeezed my eyes shut, opening them wide and squeezing them again until I could finally see Margaret laying over me. Her hips and legs disappeared between the seats, her right arm oddly twisted and bent behind her back. Blood was dripping down the side of her face, and then I knew what was blinding me.

I eased my hand under her head and tried to move Margaret toward the windshield. I couldn't budge her. Motivated by a fear I'd never known before, I forced my hands to my side and took a deep breath. With strength I didn't know I had, I managed to pull myself up to a sitting position, my back now leaning against the roof of the car. Adrenaline had dulled my pain, and I managed to support Margaret's torso while I wrestled my legs beneath me and braced my knees on the asphalt and glass below me.

Margaret's legs were wedged behind the driver's seat. I didn't have much room, working between her body and the small space between the seats where she was wedged, but my arm was long enough that I traced her leg and manipulated it until I could pull it from the space beneath my seat.

A rush of air escaped me as I eased back into the driver's area. As gently as I could, I gathered Margaret's motionless body into my arms and passed her through the windshield to the strangers waiting outside.

They took her in a flurry of activity and disappeared out of my line of sight. I had to get out. I had to get to Margaret. I had to know.

The pain was slowly returning to my ribs. It hadn't been the weight of her at all, but the fact that several of them were probably broken on my right side. Unpleasant thoughts assaulted me. The only thing that could have hit me was her…

I forced the thoughts from my mind and climbed past the steering wheel over the dash, grimacing with each clumsy move. A wave of nausea rolled over me as my hands landed on the asphalt. I pulled my legs from the car and tucked them under me, settling back on my haunches until the feeling passed.

Lifting my head, I searched the area for where they'd taken Margaret. Having separated themselves from the group, a couple of people were coming back for me. Bracing myself on my hands, I bit back the pain and forced myself upright. By then the strangers were there. They supported me, one on each side until I was standing. Once on my feet, I immediately started toward Margaret.

"Easy, man. She's bad off, but she's breathing."

His news did little to satisfy my need to get to her. I stumbled toward her, a passage slowly opening in the throng of people. Margaret lay there, covered in blood. My sweet Margaret, my renegade. I collapsed on the ground beside her, pulling her into my arms until she was cradled in my lap. Her face was so pale. Blood was still flowing from somewhere, tracing down her face and pooling on the ground. I pulled her mangled arm across her belly and folded her into me.

"Help is coming, man." The same stranger was kneeling down beside me. He pulled his shirt over his head and tucked it around Margaret's hips, covering her exposed hips and legs. I buried my face in Margaret's matted hair, listening to the sound of the approaching siren bounce off the buildings, getting closer, but still so agonizingly slow.

It couldn't end this way. The woman in my arms was my everything. My life was hers. She owned every breath I took and now…I couldn't bring myself to think it.

It felt like hours passed, and there was no sign of life from her except the shallow breath, barely felt against my body.

"They're here."

The shirtless man tapped my arm, pointing toward the street where my car had come to a stop. He helped me climb to my feet with Margaret in my arms, and I stumbled toward the ambulance.

A man jumped from the passenger seat, swooped in, and snatched Margaret away. I followed, too slow to reach the vehicle before the back door slammed shut.

"I'll take you, man. They need to go, get her to the hospital." Seconds later, the ambulance was leaving in a chorus of horns and sirens. With its departure, another group of people appeared in my field of vision, circling a man who was yelling at them.

"Don't do it." The shirtless man put his hand on my shoulder. "We need to go." I shrugged from under his touch, moving toward the crowd. My vision tunneled in on *him*, his rumpled, half un-tucked shirt, the way he staggered as he tried to find an exit from the crowd. They refused to let him go. I pushed my way through the people. I didn't need to ask who he was. The heap of metal he was standing beside told me he was the one who'd hurt Margaret.

With three feet between us, I bent at the waist and lunged into him, tackling him to the ground. As soon as our bodies stopped rolling, I was on my knees, straddling him, my fists pounding into the oozing flesh of his face.

Someone grabbed my shirt as I drew back to slam my fist into him again. I was pulled backward, but their grip failed to hold, and I surged for him again, grabbing his shirt and slamming him down on the pavement, over and over. His head cracked against the pavement. His body stilled, but I couldn't stop. I did it again.

"I've got him. I've got him." Seconds later I was again yanked from behind, and the momentum pulled me from my target. I rolled to the side, freeing myself from the grip, coming to rest on all fours and gasping for air.

"Law's here, man. We've got to go."

The man grabbed my arm and forced me to my feet, shoving me in the opposite direction of the approaching cops.

His frequent hand on my shoulder shoving me up the sidewalk kept me from turning back. That and the fact that I needed to get to Margaret. For fuck's sake. This could not be happening.

The stranger led me to an old, beat up coupe parked two blocks down. I climbed into the passenger side and dropped my throbbing head in my bloody hands. Next thing I knew, the stranger was pulling the car door open on my side.

"We're here." He reached in, shaking me from my stupor as he talked. I numbly climbed out, took in my surroundings and practically raced him to the emergency room doors.

"Margaret. Margaret Wilson." The nurse behind the counter eyed me with some apprehension.

"You kin?"

I slammed my bloody hands down on the counter. "She's my girlfriend. They brought her in a few minutes ago. We had an accident."

The nurse flipped through some papers, taking her time while I fidgeted on my feet.

"I know who she is. And I know who you are." She eyed me over her glasses. "She's in with the doctors," she said curtly. "Pretty sure she'll be going to surgery."

Her words knocked the air from my lungs. "Surgery?" I stammered.

"Why don't you go to the waiting room, and I'll send someone out to you as soon as we know more?"

Surgery. My heart flipped in my chest and took on a wild cadence. The stranger shoved me in the general direction of the waiting room. "Who do we need to call?" he asked.

My parents. I nodded toward the phone sitting over on a corner table. "I need to call my parents." My hands were shaking so bad I could barely dial the number. All I could see was the bloody prints my finger left as I pressed the buttons. Margaret's blood.

"Hello?"

The words wouldn't come.

"Hello?"

I choked.

"William?"

"Dad?" It was all I could manage before my throat closed up and the tears flowed. My strength gave way, and I felt myself sinking to the floor. I couldn't lose her now, and I couldn't bring myself to say the words. The stranger took the phone from my hand.

"This is Frank Hart. I'm at the hospital with your son."

Chapter 32 - Margaret

THE NOISE WOKE ME. An incessant beeping that interrupted my dream and pulled me from sleep, pulled me from William's arms, and landed me in a place I didn't recognize.

I was surrounded by white — white walls, a white blanket covering my body and tucked too tightly at the foot of the bed. My arm, wrapped in a white cast, lay snuggled on a white pillow at my side.

I swallowed, trying to rid the dry lump that seemed to be blocking my throat. I called to my dad, huddled sleeping in a chair in the corner, but the raspy whisper barely made it past my lips. I eased my head to the left, catching a glimpse of a rolling table. I reached my unsteady hand out to pull it to me, to make some noise to wake my dad. My eyes focused on the wood grained edge, the spot I willed my hand to go.

Control escaped me. My hand fluttered at the effort and my vision blurred. I closed my eyes for clarity, but they were just so heavy I couldn't open them again.

A woman was standing over me. A nurse with a cap pinned to her hair. She smiled at me when I noticed her and gently patted my arm.

"I'll get your father."

She faded away. I was so tired. I closed my eyes to rest while I waited for him.

"Margaret. Margaret, wake up, sweetheart."

My mother was calling me, but my eyes were so heavy.

"Come on, Margaret, talk to me."

There was fear in her voice, and it bothered me. I tried again. I wanted to talk to her. I wanted to find out what was wrong, why she was scared.

"Your dad is worried. I'm worried. Won't you wake up, please?"

I couldn't open my eyes, but my lips parted and quivered as I tried to answer her. I was awake. I heard her.

"Mom." I did little more than mouth the word, but I heard a sob escape from my mother and felt the weight of her as she hugged herself against me.

"Margaret, thank God, I've been praying every minute He wouldn't take you away from us."

I rubbed my tongue over my lips, desperate to find some moisture for my mouth. It brushed over my skin like sandpaper. "Water."

My mother sat up. "I'll go ask the nurse."

I heard her footsteps fade from the room, and I focused on opening my eyes. The bright lights of the room stung the instant I managed to pry them apart. Water pooled and cascaded down my face when I squeezed them shut again.

Footsteps approached, and I turned my head in the general direction of the sound. "Darling, she said a sip or two until the doctor sees you."

A sip or two would have to do, but I knew it would be like peeing on a fire. I needed glasses—gallons—of water to fix this thirst.

"I'm going to sit you up." I didn't recognize the voice, but the head of the bed started to rise, bringing me with it. It stopped and a cup pressed to my lips. "Tiny sips."

The woman didn't give me a choice— I had earned a small taste of the cold water before the cup disappeared. It was hardly enough to wet my tongue. "More, please." My voice, though better, still cracked with the words.

The cup reappeared against my lips. "This is it for now."

With her warning ringing in my ears, I sucked in as much water as I could before she pulled the cup away. I held it in my mouth and wet every millimeter of skin the tiny amount would wash over before swallowing it.

I felt the bed dip under someone's weight and guessed that my mother was back at my side.

"The lights…" I swallowed, trying again. "They're too bright."

"I'll turn them off on my way to get Dr. Lee."

The door clicked shut and my mother took my hand in hers. "That should be better, darling. Can you open your eyes for me?"

Once again I endured the effort. My mother rose and returned, placing a cool rag in my hand. "See if this helps."

I held the refreshing cloth to my face with my good hand and considered trying to suck the moisture from it. I needed more than the couple of sips I'd been given.

It did help and, in increments, I was able to open my eyes and peer out from behind the cloth. Squinting, even in the darkened room, my mother's worry faded to relief and a smile brightened her face.

"What happened?"

Her smile faltered, and my apprehension grew.

"Mom?"

She took a breath. "A man ran a stoplight and hit William's car."

I glanced around the room, a feeble attempt to find William at my bedside.

"Where is he?" My voice was still barely a whisper, but my mother's reaction told me she understood everything I said.

"Your father won't let him come. He's upset, Margaret. Rightfully so."

"You said…someone…hit him…us."

Mom opened her mouth to respond, but the door to the room flung open, and the doctor came in, my father close on his heels.

"Nice to see you awake, Margaret. You had me worried."

I couldn't look at him. My attention was focused on my father and the fact that he was keeping William away from me. I had to make him understand.

The doctor, who I presumed was Dr. Lee, commenced to doing some simple tests to gauge my responses. Satisfied, he pulled a rolling stool closer to my bed.

"Your brain had some swelling, Margaret. I don't want you getting up without anyone around until we're sure you're steady on your feet."

I ignored him, keeping my attention on my father who was pacing nervously at the foot of my bed.

"I'm sure you've noticed your arm is broken, but that's the least of our worries. You had some internal bleeding. We took care of that in surgery, but it's important you don't overexert yourself, or it could start again. We need to be certain you're completely healed. Do you have any questions for me?"

I didn't have to think about it. "Water?"

He chuckled, a dry sound meant to be kind. "You sure can. Small sips, though, until we're sure your stomach can handle it. We don't need you to start vomiting." He turned to my parents. "Anything else?" Neither of them spoke up. Dr. Lee stood. "I'm sure as you get over the excitement of Margaret waking up there'll be some questions we haven't covered over the last few days. I'll check back later."

With that, he left, breezing out of the room as quickly as he'd entered.

"Days?" I looked to my mom for clarification. She came back to my bed and sat on Dr. Lee's vacant stool.

"Sweetheart, the accident was a week ago yesterday. A lot has happened since then." She smiled and pulled herself closer to the bed. "I'm going to be getting treatment. Did you hear me, sweetheart? A local doctor is taking on dialysis patients, and I'm on the list."

I heard her, but I was watching my father over the rim of my cup. He was still pacing. He knew what was coming. Before I could open my mouth, the nurse breezed back into the room. "Dr. Lee sent me with your pain medicine."

I glanced around the room, confused. I wasn't hurting. The nurse, apparently ever observant, raised the syringe in her hand with an almost satisfying grin. "And this is *why* you're not hurting."

The nurse pulled the covers up from the side of the bed and with an expert hand, tilted my hip just enough to expose the area she needed for the shot. The stench of alcohol filled the room as she cleaned her target and plunged the drug into me. I looked from her to my mother and to my father who had turned his back for the process. There was something there, right on the brink of my memory that disturbed me about being exposed. A fuzzy feeling rolled over me, and I closed my eyes against the sensation. My eyelids grew too heavy to open, and a slow, muffled cadence could be heard in my ears. It was soothing and a breath later, the tension evaporated and sleep claimed me.

The room was dark when the shooting pain pulled me from my sleep. I grabbed my arm, my grip doing nothing to ease the pain through the cast. I flexed my fingers trying to stretch out the ache. It didn't help. Fumbling around the railing, I found the button that would turn the light on for my nurse. She came quickly, prepared, offering me little more than a tight smile as she cleaned and pushed the drug into me.

"How about something to drink?"

I nodded, wishing I could produce enough saliva to wash down the scratch in my throat. The nurse raised the bed and passed me the cup. She left the room as I put it to my lips, and I gave a rebellious grin at the fact that she wouldn't be there to take it away from me. I drank it down and set the empty cup on the table, looking around the room for a phone. Nothing. I pushed the cover back from the bed and eased up, letting my feet dangle over the bed. I felt a little dizzy and closed my eyes against the sudden nausea.

Cradling my broken arm in my other hand, I lay back down and buried my head in the pillow. I stayed like that a minute, collecting myself before rolling over and drawing my legs back on the bed. Getting up wasn't going to happen. I thought about William, wondering if he was here, in the hospital. Had he been hurt? I searched my fuzzy memory, trying to recall…had Mom said anything about him when I first woke up? I couldn't think. I felt like my brain was melting. I blew out a long breath and tucked my feet under the blanket. Tomorrow. Tomorrow I would fix this.

My mother was sitting by my bed when I woke. Sunlight was streaming in the one window in the room, illuminating the chair my father was resting in.

"Good morning, darling." My mother leaned in to kiss my cheek. I managed a smile and looked back to my father. "Can we talk?"

"Margaret?"

My mom's voice was edged with hurt, concern. "Sweetheart, this probably isn't the best time."

She knew where I was headed. Hesitantly, she stood, gathering her purse. At the door, she turned, nodded to me as if the meaning of the moment had come to her. A supportive smile, and she was gone.

I pounced before the door closed. "Why did you send William away?"

My dad stood, pacing back and forth, chewing on the corner of his thumb, ignoring me.

"You know, the only reason Mom is getting treatment is because of him, because of his family. How could you do this?" My throat hurt. I was straining it, but I wouldn't wait to get my point across. I pulled the rolling table to me and gulped down some water, swished it around, and drew another mouthful in.

He stopped, bracing his hands on the footrest of my bed. "We can talk about this later."

"No, we talk about it now."

He shrank away, visibly surprised at my conviction.

"Why did you send him away?"

His head began to bob, accepting that this conversation wouldn't be delayed. "Margaret, he hurt you. If it weren't for him, you wouldn't be here."

"Mom said someone hit us." My voice was getting stronger, steadier. I drank another sip of water.

"His family manufactures the alcohol that put you here." My father, hands on his hips, stood for a moment at the foot of my bed. "He was racing."

I closed my eyes, thinking back through the blackness to the last memories I could grasp.

"Not when we wrecked." I distinctly remembered William letting off the gas and the yellow Camaro sailing past us.

"He had been. With you in the car."

It was the closest my father had ever come to yelling at me. At the hotel, his anger had been tempered with disappointment. Now, his face was red, and that told me he was just short of rage, but I wasn't backing down from this.

I remembered the driver and crude gesture he'd made. I was disgusted with him for doing such a thing behind William's back. "I told him to do it."

"Excuse me?"

I swallowed, this time more from the disappointment expressed in those two words than my sore throat. "I said, I told him to do it."

My father pulled himself straight, letting go of my bed and stuffing his hands in his pocket. "It doesn't matter. He should have been taking care of you."

I snorted, amazed he was so blind with anger he couldn't see it. "*He* didn't hurt me, Dad. You think about Mom. He could have backed out of their agreement with the doctor, they could have kicked Mom out of the program. They didn't. He didn't because he knows I need my mother. He did it for me." My words were cracking again and my voice was quickly losing the headway I'd gained.

"I'll not be trading my wife for your life, Margaret."

"That is not what this is about," I argued. "You're not so angry at him that you aren't willing to accept what he offers." He stiffened, and I froze as I realized the unthinkable. "Are you going to let her die just to keep distance between us?"

There were few occasions that my father was at a loss for words. He opened his mouth to speak, but the words faltered. He resumed his pacing, and I searched for more ammunition.

"What are you going to tell Mom, that she can't get treatment because her daughter made a bad decision?"

"Margaret, stop."

He resumed his pacing. "Can you sit down a minute?"

He eyed me with some suspicion.

"I want to tell you the truth about that night, the night that started all this."

Dad pulled the rolling stool several feet from my bed. "I can't imagine anything that you could tell me that would excuse that boy's behavior."

My eyes fell shut. God forgive me, this wasn't my story to tell, but I had to make him understand. I stumbled over the words, but once I committed, the story came with ease. When I mentioned the tire iron, my dad stood, his anxiety getting the better of him, and continued pacing the room. When I finished, I brushed the tear from my cheek and looked to my dad for some sort of absolution.

Dad stopped his pacing and turned to me, his eyes wet with tears, his body slouching in defeat. He ran a trembling hand through his graying hair and then pulled it back over his face as if to block out this entire ordeal. Without a word, he turned and walked out of the room.

Chapter 33 - William

I IGNORED THE KNOCK on my door, knowing it was either Mom or Dad and that they'd come in anyway. They'd been keeping a close eye on me since the accident. They'd kept quiet about Margaret for the most part, making me feel even worse about having not introduced her to them. I couldn't even give them an honest reason why that meeting hadn't come about, except that everything about my relationship with her was low-key, comfortable, and I had wanted to keep it that way.

My father's head poked through a second later.

"Mr. Wilson is here to see you."

Too quickly I sat up, grabbing my wrapped ribs at the sudden pain my movement brought on. "What does he want?"

"To talk to you I'd imagine, son."

My father stood there watching, waiting for my decision. I hadn't seen any of the Wilsons since the night of the accident. Her dad had met me coming out of a treatment room, and after a nasty scene, insisted I leave the hospital.

"Don't think you're going to win this," I had told him as Frank pulled me from the confrontation. Mr. Wilson had just stood there, his face red with rage. Somewhere in the recesses of my mind, I understood, but there was no way in hell I was going to accept it.

By then someone had found my new friend a shirt and he dragged me back to my own treatment room. They were wrapping my ribs when my parents had burst into the room. They stopped short, the scene itself answering many of their questions. Mom took a seat in the room's only chair, and my father leaned against the wall by her side, waiting for the nurse to finish. Another, friendlier nurse stuck her head in the room.

"Margaret has some internal bleeding. They're working on getting it stopped. She's holding her own for now."

"Who?" My father pushed himself off the wall. They had no idea I was with anyone. My mother recognized the helplessness on my face and stopped him short.

Frank, who'd been holding up the opposite wall started toward the door. "I'm going to go find us some coffee."

Not a word was spoken until the nurse cleared the room. "William?"

I ignored the question in my mother's voice, looking to my father instead. "You're probably going to need to call your lawyer." I knew the cops would be there soon if they weren't already being held at bay by the staff. Not just for the racing, but because of what I'd done to the driver.

Mom came to me, taking my face in her palms. "Who is Margaret, sweetheart?"

My shoulders were shaking with restraint, but silent tears were flowing. I was folded into her arms, and my anguish was released.

At some point, my dad slipped from the room, returning some time later. Frank seemed to have disappeared altogether. The same nurse would come in once in a while, passing along updates of Margaret's surgery, letting us hang out in the treatment room well after I was ready to go home. No further questions came. I assumed my father had learned all he needed during his absence from the room and my reaction about Margaret had told Mom all she needed to know. There'd be time for more later. They knew. They were angry, but they let me lay in the bed I'd made. We finally went to leave the hospital after word came back that she was out but in a coma.

Frank had been waiting in the waiting room and stood as we walked through. I offered him my hand, and he shook it. It was the first time I'd thought to introduce him to my parents.

My father shook his hand. "I appreciate you calling us and for staying with William." My mother nodded her agreement, shaking Frank's hand.

"I'd really prefer to stay around here a little longer." My dad took a look around the room, noting the location of the Wilsons and summing up the potential for disaster. They were gone, likely in whatever room Margaret had been taken to.

"I'll bring him home," Frank offered. "It isn't like he hasn't already jacked up my night."

My father looked to me with a warning wrapped up in a question. I nodded. I could handle this, and I wouldn't give the cops a reason to be knocking on the door in an hour.

He looked back to Frank. "Get our number from William, and call if you need us."

Frank nodded, and for the first time, I wondered why he'd gotten so involved in all this. Once my parents were gone, I asked him.

"Seemed the right thing to do. If I hadn't offered, your parents would have insisted on staying. You didn't want that, did you?"

I was already shaking my head in agreement. I liked this cat.

"So, how are we going to sneak you into her room?"
I liked him a lot.

That wasn't the last time Frank helped me sneak in. He and the compassionate nurse had grown savvy about coordinating my visits, leaving me to my misery after visiting hours, and I had sat by Margaret's bed in silence, holding her one good hand in mine, willing every ounce of my strength into her, talking to her, even talking to the God she put so much faith in to. Maybe someone had told Mr. Wilson. Maybe something had changed. Had she gotten worse? Was she awake? Talking to Mr. Wilson couldn't be avoided.

"No, I need to face him. Something may have happened to Margaret."

I stood, stretching my achy body to its full height. It was hard to believe I was still so sore a week later, but the doctor had said the broken ribs would make life rough for me for a while.

My dad followed me downstairs, trailing behind me as I entered the family room. Mr. Wilson stood as I entered, eyeing my father, who I was sure lingered somewhere close behind me.

Neither of us offered anything by way of a greeting. We simply stared, two men vying for a woman in very different, but equally passionate ways.

"My daughter says she loves you," he finally said.

I nodded. "I have every intention of making sure that doesn't change."

He nodded, accepting my veiled statement that there'd be no keeping us apart.

"Her mother is…fragile…sick. Margaret will be all I have left."

I didn't know what to say to that — there were no words of comfort to offer a man who was already mourning the loss of a wife he still had, the years they'd lose. Even with dialysis, Mrs. Wilson would be taken from them long before she should be. Still, it all held no bearing that one way or the other, I would be a part of Margaret's life.

Mr. Wilson clasped his hands behind his back, bowing his head to the floor.

"It wasn't my fault, Mr. Wilson. I shouldn't have been racing with Margaret in the car, but I didn't hurt her."

He nodded again, and I surmised it was a habit born of nervousness, an act of postponement while he collected his thoughts.

"They said he might not live."

I didn't have to ask who he meant and at his mention, a fury pulsated through me so powerful that it brought a tremor to my muscles. "He climbed out of his car without a scratch. The drunk fuck deserves to die," I said, flatly.

He barely flinched at my words. Instead, his eyes met mine, and an unchristian flicker of appreciation flashed in his face, a thank you of sorts for beating the man who'd done this to his daughter, and then it was gone.

"Margaret also explained to me about Vincent. I wish you kids would have come to us. You shouldn't have had to deal with that on your own." He stalled and cleared his throat. "It's obvious you care for my daughter. She's awake and, if you're free, I'm sure she'd love to see you."

"I'll get my coat," my dad said from behind me, but my mind was still focused on what Mr. Wilson had just said and the flood of relief his words brought. I closed my eyes and raised my face to thank Margaret's God for keeping her safe. My shoulders shook with the effort of containing the sobs threatening to take me to my knees. What would I have done without her?

I pulled myself together and turned my attention back to Mr. Wilson. Ignoring my private moment, he stepped forward. He offered me his hand, and I took it.

"You two are going to be just fine," he said.

I managed a terse nod, the anger I felt at him trying to deprive me of being with Margaret still lingered, despite our truce.

Dad returned to the living room. "Your mom will be down in a minute."

I wasn't surprised. Neither of them had left the house the last few days, staying close but giving me space. They sensed I needed both, and as usual for the Steele family, we closed ranks when necessary.

"Her mother left the hospital just before I did. I'll go home and check on her and give you and Margaret some time."

"Thank you." I walked him to the door and let him out, turning to go upstairs and get my shoes and coat. Ten minutes later my parents and I were on the way to the hospital.

She was asleep when we arrived, laying on her back, her broken arm resting on a pillow and her red hair fanned out around her face like the devil's crown. My little renegade. I slipped onto the bed on her good side.

"Margaret."

She didn't move. I leaned to her ear. "Marguerite, wake up."

My parents took their seats: Mom in the armed chair and Dad on the rolling stool pushed under the shelf beside Margaret's bed.

I kissed her forehead, and her head turned toward me as her eyes fluttered open. "William."

My heart pounded in my chest at the pitiful voice that reached out to me, so different from my vivacious Margaret brimming with life. I felt the familiar rage threaten to consume me, and I stomped it down, refusing to let this moment with her be marred by anger.

I tried to focus on those beautiful green eyes, the ones that looked at me like I held the secret of life, blotting out the raging bruises and cuts she still had. "I brought some people to meet you."

"Yeah?"

I smiled. It was so like her to roll with it. She wasn't a bit concerned about pretenses. "Meet my dad, Robert Steele."

My dad took a gentle seat on Margaret's opposite side. "I hear you've been colluding with my son."

Margaret chuckled and reached for his hand with her good one. "Nice to meet you, Mr. Steele."

"No, no. Robert it is. We aren't much on formality in our family."

I laughed because it was a perfect description of us. "And this is my mother, Valerie Steele."

My father stood, offering his bedside seat to my mother. "Hi, Margaret. I'm sorry it's taken my son so long to introduce us." Mom shot me a look of disapproval before turning her attention back to Margaret. "Is there anything that you need?"

Margaret accepted my mother's fawning with her usual good nature. "An escape route, if you know one."

Mom leaned in and in a conspiratorial whisper said, "We'll work on that. In fact, since we've been confined to the house lately, Robert doesn't know it yet, but he's taking me for lunch. I'll see what we can do."

Mom stood and looked at me. "We'll be back later to take you home. If you need to, you can use my car to come back."

We said our goodbyes, and when they were gone, I adjusted myself as close to Margaret as I could get without making her uncomfortable.

"I'm guessing your Shelby is gone for good."

"Uhhmm. It's destroyed."

"No one has told me much about the man that hit us."

I tried to keep my body from tensing, but it was a useless fight. "He was drunk. He's still unconscious."

"He must have been hurt pretty bad."

I nodded, nestling my face into her hair, deciding I wouldn't be telling Margaret the details of his injuries.

"I haven't heard much about him."

Margaret eyed me, her tired eyes searching mine, but she didn't ask any questions. "You know my underwear are still in your car."

I laughed at the announcement, the first time I had since that night and it felt good. Natural. Like all was right with the world.

Chapter 34 - Margaret

WILLIAM had joined us for dinner, a random habit of his these days. Ever since I'd come home from the hospital, William had spent more and more time at our house and the fact that he was now welcome made me the happiest girl on the planet.

My mom had started her dialysis, and her behavior and health had steadily improved. It wasn't a cure, but it delayed the inevitable, and my father seemed to fight back tears every time William came around. Maybe it was a combination of things. I was nineteen now. Mom was better and the ordinary stress that had been a huge part of our days had subsided.

There was no returning to normal for William and me. It was only forward. There were no more doubts. No more questions about who he was or where I stood, only the defining moments that made us who *we* were.

He'd taken me to the diner a few times since I'd come home to get me out of the house, and even though we'd run into Victoria a time or two, it all seemed so long ago that neither of us was fazed by her haughty demeanor. She still had Anthony tagging along behind her, but rumors were rampant as always. I shrugged it off, and so did William. The truth would become obvious in a few months, but we were light years away from caring anymore.

Robert and Valerie had invited my parents and me to their home for Thanksgiving. It was the first time I met Frank, who had become a reliable and fast friend to William. He was a student at the local university, an undergrad, and overachiever who had opted to take summer classes instead of going home to Minnesota for the summer. He'd come upon the accident on his way from an evening class.

Despite the warm welcome the Steeles provided them, my parents were more comfortable in our own home than the sprawling mansion they lived in. Our families remained friendly, but there was still a divide that we hadn't bridged.

I still had some residual effects from the wreck, occasional headaches, and bouts of dizziness. My arm was healed, and except for some discoloration where the cast had been, you couldn't even tell it had been broken. Dr. Lee said my insides should be good, but warned me against strenuous activity just in case. The man who hit us remained in the hospital, and all the Steele's lawyer would say was, we'll have to wait and see.

William had finally explained to me his reaction toward the driver that night, and after the shock had worn off, we discussed what the outcomes could be and how we'd handle each. Ultimately, whether he lived or died would make the difference between an assault charge and a murder charge.

Sitting at the table with William and my mother and father in easy conversation, I couldn't help but feel we were all right where we were supposed to be.

After we had eaten, William went with my father into the living room to watch *Mayberry RFD* while my mother and I straightened up the kitchen. The banter and joyful environment we were sharing was much like it was before she got sick. With both of us working together, it didn't take us long to have the dishes done and the kitchen set back to order.

"Shall we go join our men?"

I giggled at the grin on her face and finished wiping the table. I tossed the dishcloth in the sink. "Yes, let's."

Like giddy school girls, we went to the living room. My father immediately jumped up and turned off the TV, changing the atmosphere of the room. It was too late and too obvious to keep my curiosity at bay.

"What's going on?" I asked, looking from him to William, both of them looking guilty as sin. When neither of them spoke, I walked around the couch and turned the TV back on, looking at it, dumbstruck. This was it. This was President Nixon's answer to the draft.

A board posted in the background listed numbers 1-366. They were drawing capsules out of a glass jar, birthdays, and posting them on the board in the order they were drawn.

"This is how they're assigning lottery numbers for the draft?" I asked my dad, refusing to look at William, afraid of what I would see there.

He nodded his head. "For anybody born between January 1, 1944, and December 31, 1950," he said softly. I still couldn't bring myself to look at William. Those dates put him firmly in range.

I looked back to the TV and saw that September 14 was already in the number 1 spot. "So every man born on September 14 is being drafted? When?"

A muscle in my dad's jaw clenched. I knew he didn't want to have this conversation with me. William had made it clear he wouldn't seek a deferment.

"I'd imagine the first of the year."

I sank onto the arm of the couch and turned my attention back to the TV. April 24th was drawn. December 30th. February 14th was designated 4, and I suddenly felt sick for all the men born on Valentine's Day that would be drafted, as it was, the first of the year.

October came up next, and my heart froze until the eighteenth was announced. October 18th. That was close. I didn't know how much of this I could stand to watch, but it was like a tragedy that sucked you in, made you pay attention.

September 6th. October 26th.

October 26th. A silence descended on the room. The voices from the TV faded into oblivion. My world shrank to escape the overload of emotions and my peripheral vision tunneled to an indention on the carpet where a potted plant had sat for too long. I found myself wrapped in someone's arms as I sank to the floor. No, no, no echoed in my mind, and I shook my head to dispel my thoughts.

"Listen to me, Margaret, listen."

William's voice reached through the darkness that threatened to consume me and pulled me back to him. He swept me into his arms, and little things began to seep into my awareness. A warm tear streaked my cheek. His hand brushed my hair, his fingers combed through my mass of curls. I don't know how much time passed before I became aware of my mother standing over me, her fingers pressed to her lips, tears silently falling from her closed eyes. My father was sitting in his chair, his hands folded, head bowed in prayer. I gulped in a breath and leaped from William's arms. I needed air, and I ran to the door, busting through it into the cold winter night. I braced myself against the porch rail and struggled to fill my lungs with air, an impossible task when everything I'd eaten was trying to come up.

William followed me and rubbed my back, waiting patiently for me to collect myself. I wanted to shove him away. I wanted to throw myself around him. He had so many options, and he was choosing instead to walk into the fire. *Jesus, help me.* I bent over the rail, closed my eyes, and whispered a quiet prayer of my own. When I managed to speak, I simply asked, "Why will you not run?"

"That's not a man you'd want, Margaret."

"I want you alive." I bit back a sob as the words escaped me. My hands balled into fists at my side, every fiber of my body hating him for the decision he'd already made.

"I can enlist, Margaret, avoid the draft and maybe come out a little better than most, but I won't run. You know this. Please, sit down and talk to me." William led me to the steps, and we sat, in silence, for a while. "Margaret, I need to do this knowing you'll be here when I get back."

"If you want me to give you permission to go, I won't," I snapped. "William, I can't."

He moved to the steps below me, turning to face me, taking my hands in his. "I'm not asking you to say the words, Margaret. All I need you to do is to tell me, the day I get back, the moment I return, that you'll marry me."

Tears welled in my eyes again. I closed them and let my head drop, needing to regroup.

"I'll do one tour, Margaret. I'll be home in a year, and you'll have me for the rest of your life. I swear to God; you'll never have to say goodbye to me again. Say yes."

His raw emotion tore at what was left of my heart. There was no denying him. "It was never a choice, William. It will always be just you. My future lives right here." I placed my hand on his chest. "You come home to me, and we'll finish forever, together."

Chapter 35 - William

SHE NEVER AGAIN ASKED me not to go, but it was there with every word, every kiss. I wanted nothing more than to start my life, our life, but it would have to wait. Boarding that bus was the hardest thing I had ever done.

I took a window seat, watching them through the glass. Margaret was barely holding her composure, wrapped in the arms of my mother who dabbed at her own tears. My father, his hand on my mother's shoulder, stood with his fear shrouded in pride. He could have gotten me free of this war, but since when did Steeles turn their back on a fight?

He nodded with silent approval, and I raised my hand to the cold window. My mother and Margaret refused to look, even when the bus rolled from the station. When they were out of sight, I straightened myself in my seat, months and months of the unknown ahead of me, but I had plans. They would sustain me.

Chapter 36 – Margaret The War

IT WAS impossible to cocoon myself inside my pain. The country was in turmoil with men barely more than boys being called up and torn from their families. Jobs were left vacant, and women filed in to fill them, and I was no exception. I was working along with Valerie at Steele, Inc. to keep track of the mass of men leaving for war and the applications coming in. As a matter of principle, we tried to fill each position with a family member of a soldier. A small way they could give back to the home front.

Each evening on my way home, I would stop by the office of The Sentinel, a macabre habit of reading the list. It was a redundant habit. Families were notified by the military in person, but with the number getting longer every day, surely one could be overlooked. MIA. KIA. POW. Each tag held the name of a soldier in its place, and it was with a mixture of relief and guilt that I left, having not found William's name in black and white, but recognizing others. The combined lists would be read in church on Sunday, followed by a moment of silence when the church bells would ring out through the town.

My heart ached for so much young blood spilled in swamps and jungle, but as long as it wasn't William's, I could face another day. Yet, there was no relief except the mind-numbing routine that perhaps kept me sane, even as the winter weather gave way to spring and the Earth came alive. I felt like my life was on hold, like William had ripped my heart out and carried it with him. I merely existed.

Tammy wrote toward the end of April. Vincent had not escaped the lottery, either. They would be marrying at the courthouse, and she would be coming home for the summer. Even that news did little to part the clouds that had invaded my life. I wrote her back that night, after I had finished my daily letter to William. Another mind-numbing habit that served to keep me busy, to keep me connected with him. I'm sure he couldn't care less what local gossip was, but letter after letter was mailed to him, detailing the latest restaurant his parents had taken me to, the drive there and a description of the menu. I wrote about how horrible the fish had been and how beautiful the view was. Mundane. Ordinary. Anything but war and death. That changed the day I saw Victoria.

She was sitting outside a small café that had opened on Main Street. My mindset to pass her by without conversation was forgotten when I saw she was crying, her hand rubbing her swollen belly. I sat down beside her, unsure of what to say or if I should even ask what was wrong.

"There's an officer standing outside my house," she offered. Her statement was followed by a shaky breath.

She didn't say cop. She didn't say police officer. My heart sank. "Do you want me to call your folks, have them meet you there?"

Victoria and Anthony had married when the rumors proved to be true, but he hadn't used the upcoming birth of their child to seek a deferment from the draft board. The running joke was that he was desperate to get away from her, desperate enough that he'd rather go to Vietnam than live with her.

"My parents don't agree with the war, us being there. I can't…I don't want to deal with them right now."

I knew some people were taking a pretty hard stance on our involvement, but I was taken aback that their beliefs would create a barrier to comforting their child, but I didn't press the issue.

"I can go with you."

Victoria sniffed and raised her face to the sky before turning toward me. "You would do that?"

I stood, taking her hand in mine.

The officer came to attention as we approached. Neighbors were watching, pausing in their tasks, knowing, but secretly grateful he wasn't standing in their drive. I knew this because I was, too.

Victoria slowed, and I wrapped my arm around her waist. We came to a stop a few feet from him.

"Mrs. Beckman?"

Victoria nodded.

"Could we step inside, please, ma'am."

Nudging Victoria toward the steps, I kept my arm around her while the officer fell in behind us. We were barely in the house before she turned, confronting him.

"Tell me what you have to say."

The young soldier blanched, linked his hands behind his back and straightened his spine as if he were going through a checklist. "Ma'am, I'm here to inform you that your husband has been killed in combat."

I could feel her trembling. I thought any minute she would become hysterical. But, she didn't.

"Now you've both done your duty. Get out."

The soldier started to speak. Victoria cut him off, gritting the words through clenched teeth. "Get. Out."

He cut his eyes to me. I nodded, prepared to stay. "I've got her."

"Yes, ma'am." He paused a moment more, as if he were still unsure, but turned on his heel and left. The wooden door bounced shut behind him, and Victoria stood, tears rolling down her face.

"What am I going to do? *What* am I going to *do*?"

I hugged her to me, unable to imagine what she was going through. I didn't want to. William was coming home to me. I wouldn't consider any other outcome.

A woman I recognized as a neighbor appeared at the door, and I waved her in. Others would follow. "I'm going to get her to her room. Would you mind listening out? I'm sure others will be over directly."

"Word spreads fast. I'll man the door."

I turned Victoria toward the hall as the woman started to tidy the already clean room. "Where's your room?" She nodded to the last door on the right, and I took her in and helped her to the bed. She rolled to her side, sobbing in earnest.

Pushing the door shut I went back to sit on the bed, rubbing her back until she cried herself to sleep. I sat there, thinking of the day in the store when Anthony had been so short with her. I was pretty sure he'd even pushed her. What other things had Victoria endured from him? I glanced around the room. The walls were bare. One picture on the dresser of the two together was the only evidence that Anthony had existed in this house at all.

"Margaret?"

I guess she wasn't asleep, after all. I lay back on the bed. "I'm still here."

"I've been such a bitch to you."

"None of that matters now, Victoria."

"I don't know why you even came here, but thank you."

There was no explanation I could think of either, except she needed someone, and I was there. That was how I explained it in my letter to William in the wee hours of the morning when I wrote to him, how I justified checking in on her the next day, and why I had attended Anthony's funeral with Victoria when her parents refused. Victoria's behavior is what led William to me. She'd hurt him. But, if she hadn't, I wouldn't be waiting for him now, waiting to start our life together. I felt William would understand, so checking on Victoria became another piece of my survival.

By the time Tammy came, Victoria was close to her due date, and we were past the point that I was hanging out with her because she needed me. Oddly, we needed one another, and Tammy's arrival was just another level of support. The three of us became very close, with Tammy and Victoria hanging out while I was at work. On occasion, they attended church with me, but as always, my Saturday evenings were devoted to the Steele's.

"You're going back to school, aren't you?" I asked. We were sitting at the table at Victoria's house. August was upon us, and Tammy had just announced that she'd decided at the last minute to take the semester off.

"Yes, I'm going back to school. I will be a lawyer. Somebody has to be prepared to defend these children." Tammy reached over and patted Victoria's belly.

"Oww."

Tammy shrieked back. "I didn't do anything, I swear."

Victoria laughed. "It's just moving."

I eyed her. She had laughed, but I'd been around her enough to know that it was forced. "You all right?"

She opened her mouth to answer, but she went pale just before she formed the words.

"What?" Tammy and I said in unison.

"My water broke."

I gasped. Tammy jumped up. "Hot damn, we're going to have a baby." In two seconds, the table was cleared of our drinks and the snacks were put away. "Where's your bag?"

Victoria was laughing in earnest now. Tammy was a hundred miles an hour. "In my room, by the closet."

She disappeared before Victoria even finished and reappeared moments later, the bag in her hand. "Let's get this show on the road."

"It's way too early to go."

"Your water broke," Tammy pointed out.

"But the contractions haven't started."

Tammy put her hand on her hip. "You've been walking around here all day complaining about your back hurting. Get up, and let's go have this baby."

Victoria threw her hands up in defeat and slid her chair back.

"I'm going to have to catch up with you guys after dinner."

I stood, giving Victoria a hug. "You're liable to be in labor all night. I'll check in later and probably still beat him here." I gave Victoria's belly a playful swat. "I'll have the Steeles drop me off at the hospital." It may have seemed a crappy thing to do, but his parents were my link to William, and I needed our Saturday dinners. Even if I cut it short tonight.

"Oh shoot, towels. I'll be right back." Tammy disappeared again as we made it to the front door.

"You're going to be OK."

She was about to open her mouth again when Tammy came back around, her arms laden with towels. I looked to Victoria; she looked at me, and we both laughed.

"What?"

"Her water broke," I said, "You're not cleaning a murder scene."

Tammy passed us by, pushing out the screen door, sticking her tongue out as she went. "Nothing wrong with being prepared. Get in the car." She nodded at Victoria, who scampered off the porch as fast as her body would allow.

I was right on time. The Steeles dropped me off at the entrance to the hospital, and I got to the labor ward just as Victoria started feeling the urge to push.

"Thank God you're here." Tammy seemed a bit overwhelmed. I went to the opposite of the bed and took Victoria's hand in mine.

"You hanging in there?" The look I got was evil personified. I backed away, all at once understanding Tammy's mood. "It's almost over," I said from a distance.

With a nurse's hand on her stomach, Victoria started to clench her teeth, a low hiss spraying from her lips. She was having a contraction.

"Get ready to push." The doctor had appeared and situated himself at the end of the bed. He gave a look to Tammy and me, quickly summing up the situation, and went back to his business without a word. Forty-five minutes later, Angela Rose was born. Tammy and I fawned over the tiny baby like grandparents. *Shoot, we hadn't even called Victoria's parents.*

Victoria yawned and hugged little Rose to her. "Not just yet. I'll call them tomorrow."

I didn't bother pointing out that it was already tomorrow. Her situation made me grateful for my own. The aftermath of dealing with Vincent and the situation with my own father had made me realize I was a fortunate one.

Victoria closed her eyes and began to drift off to sleep. Tammy looked like she was on her last leg. "Why don't you go on home?" I said, taking the tiny bundle from Victoria. "I'll stay with her."

It didn't take much convincing. Tammy had seen more than she wanted to see and she was swearing off having children by the time Rose was born. She collected her things, kissed me bye, and left.

Sitting in the wooden rocker, I held the baby, thinking back over everything that had happened over the past year. So much had changed. Who would have thought Victoria and I would be friends? Who would have thought I would become the kind of daughter that yelled to her parents where she was going on the way out the door?

I tried not to think about how close the wreck had come to ripping everything apart. Men were stubborn, but women were strong. It didn't matter if they were meek or God-fearing or outspoken and courageous. Love gives strength to everyone. I looked to Victoria. It would be that same kind of love that would give her the strength to raise Rose on her own, at least until the right one came along.

Calling for the nurse, I put Rose in her bassinette so she could go to the nursery. I checked on Victoria again, pulling the covers under her chin and turning off the light above her bed. Finally settled in the chair, I closed my eyes and thought of William. It would be the first night since he'd left that I hadn't written to him. So I talked. In my mind, I told him all my fears. I fussed at him for leaving me. I poured my heart out, apologizing for feeling sorry for myself and praising my love of William and his for me. Then I prayed. For Victoria. For Rose. For Tammy and Vincent, but most of all William, that he would come home to me.

It had begun to snow two hours before, and while it was beautiful, it was soaking into the ground as quickly as it fell. I turned, hearing Rose cooing in her crib. I picked up the folds of my dress and went to check on her. She had graduated to picking her head up, and she turned to me, seemingly happy with my approach. I reached in and picked her up.

"She's going to puke all over your dress."

Victoria arrived beside me, looking like a California goddess in her gold, princess dress. "Would that be sufficient reason to stay home?"

"Not if that means I still have to go."

I turned towards Tammy's voice. "You look beautiful."

She gave me a sarcastic smile. "So if I can go, you can go."

The Steeles were hosting a fundraiser for wounded soldiers. Apparently the approach of Christmas makes the general masses a little more giving and a ball had been planned, tickets sold, and dresses bought. There was no escape.

"What time is the babysitter coming?" Tammy asked.

Victoria laid Rose back down in the crib. "She should be here any minute. You ladies ready?"

"As much as I'm going to be. I'm going to get my purse." I went to the spare bedroom Tammy and I had used to dress and collected my things. We had dressed here to help Victoria get ready and deal with Rose, too. She'd been a little colicky and not sleeping well.

I went back to the living room just as the taxi arrived. I went out to stall, passing the neighborhood girl who would be watching Rose while we were gone. I gave her a smile and went on to the taxi, explaining the others would be out soon.

He gave me a grunt and turned the meter on. I rolled my eyes toward the house just as Tammy and Victoria stepped onto the small porch. A few minutes later, we were gone.

"This might be fun."

Tammy gave Victoria a disgusted look. "Every man that isn't old, disabled, or a coward is in Vietnam. What's your idea of fun?"

"Frank will be there." A long and well-documented history of asthma had gotten Frank disqualified. He'd been a steady visitor in my life, I'm sure at William's request, but he'd certainly not made a pest of himself.

"Pfft. He's not exactly for Victoria," Tammy said.

"Who is then, Miss Know-It-All?" I asked.

Tammy thought about it for a minute. "I'm not sure just yet."

We all laughed and spent the rest of the trip discussing who would and wouldn't be coming, who would be wearing what and who they'd bring. It was all very pre-war feeling, right up until we pulled into the driveway.

"This is gorgeous." Victoria was ducking low so she could see out the windshield.

"The Steeles rented it for the party," I explained. "It's got a huge wrap around porch that was perfect for tables, maybe even dancing."

"Too bad it's thirty degrees outside."

Victoria gave Tammy a playful slap. "It's still gorgeous. Victorians are so nice when they're all lit up like this."

Climbing out of the cab, I had to agree with Victoria. The Steeles had outdone themselves, but I didn't expect anything less.

We quickly made our way inside, leaving our coats at the door and stepping into the massive open floor plan. A string quartet played from the landing on the second floor, close enough for the melody to be heard, but far enough away that conversation and laughter could still be had. Hurricane lanterns and candles littered every surface that could hold them. The scent of fresh flowers was thick in the air.

"I should probably go find Robert and Valerie." I excused myself and made my way through the crowd, smiling politely at acquaintances and the few strangers that mingled in small groups. I found them toward the back of the room, engrossed in conversation with the mayor. They smiled and waved, Valerie pulling me into a hug when I approached.

"You look beautiful, sweetheart. Have you seen your parents? They got here about twenty minutes ago."

"No, but I just got here."

Mayor Johnson held out his hand. "I hear you're in for quite a night, young lady."

I smiled, despite my confusion. I was about to question his information when he nodded toward something behind me. "I believe your parents are wanting your attention."

I spun around, seeing my mother first, absolutely gorgeous in her black gown, on the arm of my father. It was the man who stood to her left that had me feeling faint. William stepped forward, pulling his hand from his pocket. He eased to his knee and looked up at me.

"You promised me the day I returned... Margaret Wilson, will you marry me?"

The room blurred through tears. My lungs failed. My hands flew to my face to hide my shock from the mass of people who had paused to watch the moment. I found myself wrapped in his arms, hugged, relieved, overwhelmed. Protected.

"I've missed you so much, Marguerite. I won't survive another day, another night without you."

William's raspy admission in my ear brought a fresh wave of tears. I couldn't find my voice, but I knew that I was never letting him go again. My arms flew around him.

"Yes." It was all I could manage and all William needed to hear. His lips pressed against my wet cheek.

"I promised you forever, Marguerite."

I unfolded myself from William's arms and found my life, my world, reflected in the way he looked at me. "We do forever, together."

Chapter 37 - William

MARGARET—DANCING IN MY arms—was life reborn. We said our vows in front of our families and guests, but tonight was about Margaret and all the things I owed her.

She'd danced with her father, with my father. I waited as long as I could to steal her back. I held her in my arms. "Do you approve of your house?"

Margaret's head raised from my chest. "Our house?"

I nodded. "My mother and Frank have been busy."

"This is ours?"

Her body had gone still in my arms. "Isn't this what you wanted?" I asked. Our conversation at the park about dreams had planted the seed for all this, but Margaret's whimsical letters had led us here, to this house, the wedding. It was a lifetime of dreams and desire mapped on tear-stained paper.

Margaret looked around her as if she were seeing her surroundings for the first time. Her gaze returned to me. "Everything I want is right here."

I dipped my head, agreeing. My lips found hers and a low moan rose from her.

"Is there a bed upstairs?" she whispered.

I nodded, a sly smile spreading across my face. My little renegade. Thank God some things never change.

"Let's go," she whispered.

The look on my face was more need than shock. It had been a couple of hours since we'd said our vows. "And leave our guests?"

Margaret pulled my arm up and, despite that I wasn't wearing a watch, said, "It's time for them to go, anyway."

I took her by the hand and pulled her up the staircase. Halfway up, I stopped, waving to those still mingling. "Goodnight, everybody."

Without waiting for a response, I pulled Margaret the rest of the way up the stairs and into our new bedroom. I closed the door behind us and pulled Margaret into my arms, my lips landing on hers with such need that I didn't know if I could contain myself.

"William, wait. William."

"What?"

"I have to pee."

I laughed, releasing her. "You've got one minute, and then I'm coming in after you." I pointed to the door that would lead her to the bathroom. "Hurry up."

Margaret took off across the room, and I used the time to light the candles that Frank or my mother had placed around the room. It really was magical to be back. Margaret was mine. Forever, together.

I had just sat down on the bed when she came out. She hesitated, looking around the room before her attention landed on me. She came to me, edged her way between my knees, and I was reminded of a time so long ago in my room, before life had gotten in the way.

Resting my head on her stomach, I couldn't believe I was back, that she was mine, and that my time in Vietnam was behind me. Nothing was ahead but me and her. I'd die to make it so.

Her hands landed on the back of my head, gently pressing me to her.

"Are you all right, William?"

I shook my head. I didn't know if I would ever be all right after the things I'd done, the things I'd seen. But, I would be better, with her.

Her fingers lifted my chin, and her eyes searched mine. "Look at me, William. Always look to me."

Blinking back tears, I eased Margaret from me. "I need you."

Margaret nodded and turned, pulling her hair to the side. I eased the zipper of her dress down to her waist, pushed the silk over her shoulders, and watched it pool at her feet. I unsnapped the bra she wore and pulled her down onto my lap before pushing it off to the pile. I pulled her against me, running my hands along her bare skin. She turned, claiming me as her own, and I gave in as she pushed me back on the bed.

I rolled over onto her, maintaining our kiss, my breath, my life. I loved this woman with everything I had and then some. Sliding from her, I shed my clothes and discarded them on the floor. I crawled back on the bed, drawing Margaret's warm body to mine.

"I love you, Margaret."

I stifled her response with another kiss, a need. I couldn't get enough. My lips went from hers, to her chin, nipping her neck. Her gentle moans stretched over the months that had passed and brought me back to her. My tongue circled her nipple and Margaret arched into me, calling to me as only she could.

My hand slid down her belly while my tongue and teeth explored her, taking note of each reaction and subtle tell that I owned her, that she was mine, mind, body, and soul.

When my fingers swept over the wet underwear she still wore, I brought my attention back to her face, the look in her eyes, the desire I saw there. I slipped my hand beneath the elastic and brushed my fingers over her skin, trailing the proof of her desire down the inside of her thigh. I wrapped the flimsy material around my fist and yanked. It gave way, and I tossed the ruined material on the floor.

I cupped her in my palm. "I need to be right here."

Margaret didn't speak, but she tugged me on top of her, and I gladly obliged, needing to feel her, to have her.

"This isn't going to last very long, Margaret. I need you."

Her eyes sought mine in the glow of the room and, reading, searching and accepting the tangle of emotions she found. "So take me."

My lips crashed down on hers again. It couldn't go like this. Not after all this time. "You first. It will always be you first, Marguerite." But, my body couldn't take it anymore. I pulled my knees up, forcing Margaret to open her legs to me. My hips were slowly rocking against her, and I could feel her desire drenching me.

"Tell me you need me, Marguerite." The woman in my arms was my salvation, and desperation was pouring out of me. I wanted to wait. I wanted this perfect, but if I was going to be saved, I needed her now.

"I need you, William."

I entered her with a sob. It was the moment my soul slammed back into my body, and I became whole—a man again. Her warmth and goodness enveloped me and all at once, I was forgiven; for leaving her, for every shot I'd fired while I was gone, for the lives I'd taken and the pain I'd created. Margaret loved me, and I consumed it like air.

Margaret moaned and bucked against the intrusion, crying out, releasing the pain that seeped from my body to hers. I dug my arms under her shoulders, cupping her head in my hands. "I'm sorry. I'm so sorry."

She pressed her face to mine, wrapping her arms around me and pulling me close. It was redeeming. Freeing. Her acceptance of me would be all the salvation I would ever need.

Margaret pulled my face to hers, bringing her lips to mine. She was all that mattered, and my body instinctively pushed inside her, needing more, wanting more.

I rolled over, pulling Margaret on top of me. "Open your knees." She did, and I shoved her hips down as I pushed inside her, bringing her to an angle I knew would satisfy her. The moan that rose from her was pure music, and I did it again.

The candlelight was reflecting off of Margaret's face. Her beautiful green eyes, staring so lustful into mine was a mindfuck by itself. Being buried inside her while her body clenched around me was Goddamn Heaven, if I never made it there.

"Like that, Margaret?"

She didn't have to answer. Her body seized, and her head dropped. My name drifted from her lips. I raised my hips from the bed, forcing her body against mine so that her weight held her against me. My hands on the curve of her hips pushed her down on me, rocking her in a steady rhythm that would take her over the edge.

Margaret was there, and I put my hand on the small of her back, forcing her against me until I felt the warmth of her orgasm wash over us. I rolled her over, gliding my hips against her. The panting in my ear, the pure desire that passed from her to me brought me to the point of no return. With a final thrust, I let it all go, releasing months of pain, months of missing her, months of thinking about this moment.

My entire body was trembling. I buried my head in her hair, burying myself inside her. "Don't ever let me go." The emotion spilled out of me, and I gathered her into my arms. I couldn't stop the pent up tears. Margaret held me in her arms, her hands sliding over me, my body nestled against hers, like it should be—like it *would* be.

It seemed like hours passed before I was willing to put any distance between us. I eased to my side, not missing the deep breath she seized once my weight left her.

"I squished you."

Margaret managed to get closer than she already was. "It was worth it."

My lips found her cheek, her nose, my hand squeezing the flesh of her waist. "It hardly feels real."

"I can't believe you pulled all this off. Frank hasn't said a word.

I grunted, happy that our plans had come together. Frank was a good guy. The best. He'd been my eyes and ears on Margaret while I was gone. I hadn't been happy about the whole Victoria situation, but I didn't feel like it was my place to tell Margaret it wasn't appropriate. Besides, people change, and I could tell from her letters she was completely in love with the baby.

Pushing the thoughts away, I gathered Margaret into my arms. This is where she belonged, where I needed her to be. Her lips landed on my chest, and her fingers fluttered down my stomach.

"Is there a huge backyard?" she asked.

"Umhmm."

"And trees to shade the swing?"

"Yes."

Margaret's leg crossed my hips, and she hovered over me, her hair brushing lightly against my chest as her face inched closer to mine. "Then we better get started on those children. Get it right, and he'll be here by summer."

"Get it right?" I laughed.

"Yes," she whispered, her lips raking over mine.

I returned her kiss before flipping her over, pinning her to the bed with my body. With her wrists clasped in my grip, I brought them above her head.

"How do you know it'll be a he?" I asked. "Maybe I want a girl."

"Boy first," Margaret argued, pressing her hips into mine.

"Are we negotiating again, Marguerite?"

She shook her head, grinning. "It's not negotiable."

My eyes fell shut as I slid inside her, the soft intake of her breath in my ear. It was a moot argument. It was all insignificant. I'd already won.

Epilogue - Margaret

MY EYES DANCE AROUND THE table and, for the life of me, I can't seem to settle on any one conversation. A confusing cacophony of voices drift to my ears, yet, I smile. I glance to my husband and my smile grows. This man, William Steele, he makes my heart melt even after forty-five years of marriage. He was my first, he will be my last and our children, though now grown, have been everything in-between.

William catches my gaze, and I see it, the flicker of amusement at the chaos holidays bring to our home, before it's hidden again behind the cloak of broodiness that is his norm. His right eye drops in a wink and my head tilts in mock frustration before I catch the subtle tell and straighten myself. I hope, with every fiber of my being, that our children capture this…this glorious type of love for themselves. It's a haven unto itself, a place to escape for protection and rejuvenation.

I look to Trinity, my youngest child, my only daughter. She is the physical image of me, yet she carries the personality of her father as strongly as our boys. Her engagement to Tim has unraveled, and though I'm sure she grieves, she sits here with her head held high, a strong and determined young woman.

Aiden is eyeball deep in his residency and only has eyes for his patients. There's been a nagging voice in my head that there's more going on in his life than he's willing to share, but for now I accept that he's just not ready to share this with us.

Carson, on the other hand, collects women like a child collects marbles or baseball cards. He seems allergic to relationships, and I'm afraid his personality is well-suited for his exploits. Of all the boys, Carson is the most outgoing. He's energetic and has a way of putting the people around him into a comfortable trance. Not a trait I'm proud that he possesses, but it's *him*, just the same. He is the polar opposite of Riker.

Our oldest is most like his father, so it seems that only I am yet aware of how strong, how deep, his ability to love could be. Maybe he isn't yet aware of it. Ever since we lost Eric, Riker has fumbled with his emotions. He is the one I worry about the most. He is truly his father's son, not even aware of the great gift he's so reluctant to share. He worries me and I fear that he, the one who needs it the most, will reject it when it comes.

I pick up my tea and focus again on my husband, my glass hiding the frown that I'm now unable to displace. We've been one for so long I doubt our ability to survive without the other. I stumble, and he supports us both. I breathe out, and he breathes in. We *are* us, yet, as strong as the ties are that bind me here, my body is growing tired, and I can feel this world slowly releasing me. The years are blinking by, and I know in my heart that the dawn is upon us where William will open his eyes, and there, alone, he will stand.

Excerpt From Mercy Denied

Learn more about Margaret and William through the eyes of their children in **Mercy Denied**, the first book in the Steele Standing Series.

Trinity Steele isn't a stranger to the game. Before her engagement, she played with the big boys and excelled at loving and leaving. It should be no different after she finds herself single, again.

But, this time she's seduced the wrong man for the wrong reasons, and it just might cost her everything.

Merrick wants to destroy her for what she's done. He wants to love her for believing in him. His pain and confusion has him spinning out of control, but is her faith in him enough to save her from his revenge, or will his demons destroy them both?

CONTINUE READING FOR AN
EXCERPT FROM MERCY DENIED

Prologue - Merrick

I THOUGHT THE FLOWERS were a nice touch, but Ella was looking at them like the cut crystal vase would make the perfect weapon.

"An apology?" The look on her face warned me that I was pissing in the wind.

"From the great Merrick Kincaid?" she spat, twisting the knife again.

I should have expected the anger. Lord knows I'd given her enough reason over the last few months to take my apology and shove it back in my face. Even knowing this, my attempt to brace myself failed, and my strength wilted under her words.

"I'm trying here, Ella."

Disgusted, my wife shoved her chair back, snatched her plate from the table and stomped to the sink. She dropped it in, sandwich and all, letting it clang against the stainless steel with such force that I was surprised it didn't break.

She spun around, crossed her arms over her chest and leaned against the counter. In the stark light of the kitchen, the stance only accentuated how painfully thin she was, how tired and vulnerable she looked. It was almost like her growing belly was pulling her skin taut, stretching it over her boney frame in a grotesque version of her former self.

"Let me tell you what *I'm* trying to do, Merrick."

A knot of tension formed in the pit of my stomach. My grip tightened around the arm of the overstuffed teddy bear that dangled at my side. The nails of my free hand dug into the flesh of my palm.

"I'm listening," I gritted, trying to keep my mind open and my temper in check. My delay in facing this entire situation had just about eroded our ability to be civil to each other.

"As soon as this baby is born—" she unfolded her arms and pointed to her bulging stomach with both index fingers "—I'm going back to Louisiana."

I blinked, shocked. "No."

Ella laughed at my dazed response; a tired, lonesome sound that mocked me and my sudden distress.

"*Yes*, Merrick."

She flicked a strand of her brown bob behind her ear and took in a deep breath. "Look, you're angry, and I'm trying very hard not to be. I'm sick of being angry all the time. I know you didn't want this marriage any more than I did, but you haven't exactly helped make it bearable."

I swallowed hard. We'd come to yet another fork in the road, and I could feel Ella drifting off in a direction that would take her and our baby away from me. Would there be no absolution for the choices I'd made? The words I'd said?

"I wasn't angry with *you*, Ella, I was just angry." That was the truth, but even the soft admission brought no hint of redemption to her demeanor. We had been so close. She'd been my best friend—loyal, attentive and knew me better than most. My anger about the baby…it was the blade that severed all of that and sent us each falling into our own abyss.

I was angry at myself because, even though I knew there was no future for us, I had continued to seek Ella out. We'd played this game for years. Being a normal, hormonal boy, as in thinking with my cock, I hadn't thought twice about sex with Ella. We'd been constantly thrust together on trips and the frequent visits her family made to Georgia from Louisiana. It was logical to my teenage mind that we should be together. Ella was responsive to my advances, if not enthusiastic, and I took full advantage of having her at my disposal, as well as the distance that separated us. It was ideal having someone to spend time with, but we were far enough apart that I didn't feel…obligated to her.

"We can work through this," I told her, swinging the teddy bear up, as if bringing it to her attention would break her. She shook her head.

"This was wrong from the beginning. Everyone but our parents knew it, Merrick."

She was right. Even our parents had picked up on and played into our quasi relationship, talking about our happy ever after, how our purported marriage would be a legal, if not familial way to seal our father's fraternal bond. What had started out as a convenient fuck had become a living breathing nightmare, and Mariah and I had played right into it.

The first time I realized we had dug ourselves into a hole was when I had off-handedly mentioned that I had asked Kelly McPhearson to my senior prom. My dad calmly shut his laptop, laced his hands together and laid them on his desk.

"How do you think Ella is going to feel about that?" he asked.

In the span of one comment, Ella had gone from being a fun and reliable fuck to poisoned fruit. I hadn't really given a damn how Ella felt, and I had told him so. A full-blown argument ensued, and I ended up sneaking off with not only Kelly, but every other girl that caught my attention. The older I got, the easier it was.

The teenager in me had no issues with taking a bite from the forbidden. Being with Ella wasn't exactly meteor showers and exploding rockets, but she was no chore either. In my life, where accolades surrounded me like oxygen, my father always seemed to be the one announcing his disappointment and strangling my self-worth. Ella saw this and was his polar opposite, the only one to negate his summation of how I never measured up.

As I got older, started college, and began thinking about where I was going with my career, it occurred to me that my relationship with Ella seemed to be the only area of my life that my dad approved. He would ramble on, bruising my ego at how my success—in his eyes, at least—seemed to be linked to her. Those moments had been a breath of life for my drowning ego, and I had clung to them like a scared little boy. I could see that now.

"Can we talk about this?" I was one breath away from begging when Ella sat down, tossing her hands into the air. "What do you have to say that you haven't already made clear?"

It was a harsh blow, but no less painful than the horrible things I'd spat off to her when I found out she was pregnant. This whole fiasco should have been brought to a screeching halt years ago. Once I had put college behind me, I had the freedom to travel the world while handling KP's business. To the business world, I was the prodigal son: smart, efficient, hard-working and took no prisoners when it came to moving KP, Inc. forward. Ella was still in college then and had plans for law school. With the distance between us, it was easy to ignore the growing interest our parents had in our future. In my mind, I guessed our family's expectation would change with time, but then, Ella and I gave them little reason to think it would. Habits and hormones die hard, and each time our families came together, I sought her out like a predatory cat too long caged from its prey.

It all seemed manageable at first. I had the adoration, or at least the attention, of my father for the first time in my life. None of the rest seemed real as I took on more and more responsibility, my father feeding me his approval piecemeal. While his faith in me seemed to grow, so did the opportunities to be away from his vigilant eyes. It was all very tolerable, right up until the Atlanta Business Journal put me on their cover and the article mentioned my bachelor status. Two days later, news of my engagement to Ella was leaked to the papers. It was news to me and suddenly, shit got real.

I shook my head. "This is *not* what I want."

"What isn't, Merrick? Me? Our marriage? We already know how you feel about the baby."

It was a devastating blow. The shock of Ella's pregnancy had worn off and the new reality that was to be my life had begun to bring a smile to my face. Images of parks, little league playoffs, and championship trophies filled my imagination. All the things my childhood lacked. My father raised a successor, not a son, and I didn't want that for my child. At that point, I'd even take tutus and princess parties.

"I get it." Ella held her palms out to me, bringing me back to the present. "I wasn't happy about this either, Merrick. Not after we had agreed to tell our parents to fuck off."

Pulling a chair out from the small breakfast table, I collapsed into it, pulling the bear into my lap. I had been hoping to come home and make some peace with Ella about our marriage, about our baby. It had been a long few months, but I had come to terms with it and now she was ripping apart my newfound state of mind.

"What about the baby?" I asked quietly. I had felt it move and now it wasn't unusual to see an elbow or foot or some other body part bulge against Ella's belly and zoom against her skin as the baby shifted position. Freaky as hell at first, but the visual and physical moving of my child in her belly had brought on a powerful shift in my way of thinking.

Ella sat down in the chair opposite of me and folded her arms on the table. "I'm not trying to keep the baby from you, Merrick. If you've honestly decided you want to be a father, then we'll just have to figure out how to make this work from a distance. It's the best I can do."

I didn't have to think about how I felt. My nuts had finally dropped, and I was leaving my father's company. I had grown, in more ways than one, and I found that I no longer needed the attention or approval by which I had judged my self-worth for so long. I would store my wanderlust until I was hit with empty nest syndrome and dedicate my life to being the kind of man Ella and our child could be proud of. I'd even approved renovations for updating my grandmother's farmhouse.

It seemed imperative to move my growing family out of the city and the farm was the perfect place to raise our child. My grandmother had a passion for horses and though I kept a few, I had my eye on a stud that just might make a name for himself and the farm. Even if he didn't, I had my trust fund, and I had inherited my mother's half of Kincaid Properties.

Ella wasn't a city girl, and I had felt that moving away from the chaos of the city would improve her disposition. I had hoped to give Ella time to recuperate and then surprise her. Now it was all for naught. My heart splintered at the reality and desperation flooded the void.

"Why don't you stay? We can make this work, Ella. It's not like I don't care for you."

An unmistakable shadow crossed over her. "Merrick, I'll die if I stay here." She swept her arms around her, and I instinctively took in the environment that surrounded us. It was plain, void of color and warmth. No artwork decorated the walls of our home, no smiling pictures to remind us of the important things in life. Still, I knew in my heart, all of that wasn't what she meant.

"I've known you since I was born, but I don't want to grow to hate you. This just isn't what I want."

"Tell me what that is, Ella." I was sure I could provide it.

Her face darkened. She hesitated, bowing her head. "Merrick, I'll never be happy married to a man."

She let the words sink in.

"But Ella…" words escaped me.

"Don't, Merrick. I enjoyed being with you, I mean, look at you. You're handsome and you're hot. I love you, probably the same way you love me, but, the truth is, I had met someone a long time ago, and I tried to be happy about this, to make this work, but in my heart, I'm with her. That's where I need to be."

She let her words sink in before getting up. She calmly disappeared from the room, letting the weight of her words shove me further into my despair.

What the fuck just happened? I came home today intent on starting over, making amends and setting our marriage on the proper road. For the benefit of our child, yes, but no one would ever convince me that it was for anything but the right reasons.

I sat the teddy bear on the table and my stomach twisted as I thought back on the horrific things I'd said to Ella, back when I was panicking because of the suffocating walls closing in on the freedom I had enjoyed…the now unthinkable suggestions I'd made.

Maybe doing the "right thing" had been an outdated and unrealistic approach to doing the right thing, but my mind couldn't—wouldn't—reconcile that with Ella's admission.

The nursery was complete, and I walked to it and placed the bear in the corner of the crib. There was little I could do to change Ella's mind, the situation being what it was; I didn't have the heart to try. The day may not have played out like I would have had it, but distance would not deter me from being a kick ass father.

Chapter 1 - Trinity ~ September

I GROANED AT the sound of the doorbell echoing through my apartment. I had hoped Melanie would forget our plans to go out—that a better offer would come through and distract her or a freakishly early snow storm would bring the city to a halt. No such luck.

I opened the door and stepped aside as my best friend stormed in.

"You're not ready," Melanie observed. She turned, hands on her hips and glared at me.

"Nope." I pushed the door shut from where I stood and wondered if pain in the ass friends would make a suitable murder defense. Marching across the hardwood floor to the couch, I snatched up my hot-pink blanket and settled back into the warm black leather.

"I was hoping you wouldn't come."

Hurt, Melanie threw her arms out to the side and her mouth dropped in sync like a programmed toy. "You have been moping around here for weeks. No more."

"Nobody is moping. I just don't want to go to that hole-in-the-wall you're trying to drag me to." I fluffed the matching hot pink pillow and adjusted it as I laid back down, cuddling further under my blanket and wishing she'd just go away.

Melanie and I were complete opposites. She was vivacious, outgoing and fun. She was also the quintessential, tall, blonde bombshell…all things that I was not. I was the introvert, quiet and thoughtful, with unruly red hair and on top of that, I was short. I never did grow tall enough to stretch all that baby fat into a sleek, toned body. And, while she had the ability to roll with life's punches and recover with a firm, "fuck it", I tended to brood over things. Imagine that, a Steele being broody.

We met in college, during our obligatory freshman year on campus. We were assigned as roommates and Melanie's eclectic taste in music immediately clashed with my strictly country playlist. We had both bitched and bragged about getting an apartment and getting away from each other as soon as we put that first year behind us, and we did. But, we had also become and remained the best of friends. Melanie wasn't going to ditch me. I could hope, but it wasn't going to happen.

Melanie took a seat at the opposite end of the couch. "You're really not going to go? If this is about Tim, don't think he's sitting at home crying over you. Not when he was having such a dandy time getting his dick wet in Daytona."

My insides cringed at the mention of Tim. Thank you, Melanie, for pouring salt in my gaping wound. "Christ, you'd think you were a psychology major." It wasn't meant as an assault on me, but the knife twisted in my back just the same.

She snatched away my cover. "Get up. We have a date."

"Can't we just make it a night in?" I groaned.

Melanie kicked off her shoes and tucked her feet under her. Her demeanor had softened, but her tone remained firm and uncompromising.

"Look, I get you're hurt, but I'm about to lose you to this whole foundation business, and I'm not going to let Tim ruin it for me. Goodbye carefree days of youth. So, you win by association. We are going to Simon's."

Simon's was a trendy lounge tucked in the basement of the Carter Hotel; Melanie's favorite local band was playing there. She had secured us a room, promising me a night to make me forget about Tim's betrayal. I just wanted to stay home and continue to pretend the whole fiasco had never happened. How stupid could I be?

Melanie was relentless, and I was caving. I'd spent three weeks mourning my relationship with Tim. Wasn't that three weeks longer than he deserved? Not that I'd ever give him the pleasure of knowing I'd spent a single night at home pouting over him.

He was already immersed in corporate America when he'd tagged along on our summer vacation on the pretense of spending time with me. Yeah, right. Lucky for me, I had already graduated and didn't have to face the gossip mongers who would spread the humiliation like spiked punch.

My closest friends knew the truth about why I no longer wore the gaudy diamond ring and they respected me enough not to go on about it. I'm sure Tim's mother had purchased it to ensure it lived up to the family's opulent reputation. Tim was long gone, but the scab of humiliation was scraped off on the rare occasion that a random someone would ask about the "big day". Perhaps some lucky fisherman would one day find it in the belly of a swordfish.

"Get up!" Melanie's command broke off my musing. In an awkward move, she shoved her feet behind me and started pushing me off the couch, effectively motivating me to move my ass.

Shoving myself up, I surrendered. "OK, OK."

Swinging one leg over the other, I let my black pump fall from my heel. "I'm so glad you convinced me to come," I conceded, looking around.

The inside of the place was painted black and was void of color except a blue neon sign—tactful as far as neon goes—that hung on the back wall spelling out the name of the place and served to remind those who had too much to drink where they were. There were no pool tables, no dart boards, just a small dance floor off to the left-hand side where a small stage allowed the entertainment to look out over the crowd. Tall, well-spaced tables lined the walls and a mix of couches and deep, overstuffed arm chairs created additional seating. Sturdy, oak, coffee tables gave those who chose to sit in the cozier settings somewhere to put their empty bottles. A U-shaped bar lined the right side of the room, breaking off at the entrance to a hallway where the restrooms were.

Strategically placed recessed lighting made the room bright enough to be functional, but dark enough to make you feel hidden from...well, whatever demon you were trying to drink away.

The place was usually mellow and quiet, but tonight the band had brought their own crowd, and the vibe in the room was already electric. They had a following, and even though they hadn't started playing yet, I was having a good time.

Melanie pushed a basket of wings in my direction. "Eat," she instructed. "We will drink, dance, and be happy tonight."

"Yes, ma'am." I gave her a wide smile, emptied my shot glass and selected a wing from the basket.

"Ohh," Melanie slammed her palm on the table, excited. "How long do you have before you take over the shelter?"

I rolled my eyes. Melanie always referred to my mother's foundation as 'the shelter,' but it was so much more. The Steele Standing Foundation was a hodgepodge of community programs, outreach centers, and food banks. The shelter was just the physical hub of a very intricate societal and familial machine. Mom had dedicated her life to it. It was my mother's baby, and I grew up working side by side with her as she nurtured it. Now, she was preparing to hand it over to me.

"Nothing is official until the first of the year. Everything from now to then is negotiable."

I sucked the sauce from my fingers and settled back in my chair, pulling my Heineken in reach. Unlike Melanie—who was tall and leaned her frame against the seat—I'm short at barely 5"2'. For me it was on the stool, or off it.

"Think we could squeeze in a trip to Vegas?" Melanie asked, her perfectly paid-for capped teeth shining in the dim room.

I shrugged, feigning distraction by the band tuning up on stage.

"Maybe," I hummed, reconsidering the possibility. "It might be fun."

Melanie lunged across the table and threw her arms around me. "That would be so awesome. One last kick-ass trip."

Twenty minutes later and another shot of tequila in, we were on the dance floor bouncing around to the beat of the music. Melanie sang along to every song, and the energy of the crowd was contagious, but the steady beat of grunge rock just wasn't my thing, and I needed a break. I grabbed Melanie's hand and led her back to the table.

"Are you ladies giving up so soon?"

We turned, eyeing the two frat boys that had followed us to our seats. Melanie groaned. "Not tonight, boys. Get going." Raising her hands, she wiggled her fingers, sending them on their way.

Climbing back up on my stool, I accepted a new beer from the waitress. As she walked away, my gaze was drawn to the man who filled the entrance. He paused to let his eyes adjust, or perhaps to survey the seating, before making his way to the bar. He took a seat at the corner on one of the few empty stools between the bar and the wall.

Melanie grabbed my arm and leaned across the table.

"Holy shit. Do you know who that is?"

She had distracted me—scared me, actually. I refocused my attention on him, but I couldn't place him. He wasn't the kind of man a woman would forget. He looked young, but he carried himself with an assurance born of world experience. He looked neither left nor right as he had traversed the room and the crowd seemed to part for him as he made his way to his seat.

I found myself not wanting to look away from him so I shook my head, keeping my eyes on him. Shameless, I know, but how could someone with such mass move with such grace? Even in the dim lighting, I could see that his tailored suit did nothing to hide his physique. If anything, it accentuated it. There was definitely a treasure under all that wrapping.

The lighting at the bar, with the reflection of the lights in the mirror, was better than anywhere else in the bar, and once he took his seat, his features came into focus. He turned his head, glancing around the room, giving me a full view of his beautiful face and there it was…a sudden weight in my chest. I raised my bottle, averting my eyes.

"That's Ella's husband."

I coughed up the beer I'd been swallowing, gagging on air, beer, and disbelief. I turned my attention back to Melanie.

"That's him? Are you fucking serious?" I asked. My words were more like gasping questions, but she interpreted them just the same.

While I had met Ella, she was technically Melanie's friend. I liked her, we just never clicked in the way friends do, so she remained on the fringes of my life through Melanie. I'd certainly never met her husband. Ella was older than us, in law school, and mentored Melanie because visions of law school danced in her head. They'd hit it off and Ella had been helping Melanie with some of her more difficult classes, advising her on applying, and had been there to ensure that Melanie was on the right road.

Ella had been in her third year of law school when she got pregnant. No one had really raised an eyebrow about that, but the whispers started when she left school. I knew even less about her husband, except that the man was considered southern royalty, yet Ella seemed to be the only one not enthralled by him. I didn't get it.

Merrick was a couple of years older than Ella and, despite their…relationship…had apparently been enjoying the single life right up until he'd been painted as Georgia's most eligible bachelor. Days later, the same columnist broke the hearts of many a debutante by unofficially announcing their engagement.

Melanie was one of the few people who had seen him in the flesh. Ella never talked about him, she was never seen with him yet, they had always just…been, and she certainly didn't glow with the radiance of a woman in love. It was the oddest damn thing.

"That's him, all right." Melanie nodded, her perfectly-plucked, blond eyebrows bunching together. "That fucker needs his balls cut off."

I couldn't help but laugh. "I never understood that whole situation anyway." I wasn't sure I wanted to.

Pulling her chair closer, Melanie firmly planted herself in her seat. Her blue eyes sparkled with anger and, I was certain, the alcohol. "I don't know the whole story. Ella has disappeared. She won't return my calls. The phone says my texts are read, but she won't answer those, either."

Melanie's tone was edged with sadness, and my distrust for the man multiplied.

"I haven't talked to anyone who's seen or heard from her," Melanie continued. "Word is she went back to her family in Louisiana."

Melanie didn't give me a chance to ask questions, but it all seemed a little dramatic to me. For Ella to give up on all that she'd worked for? It just seemed a bit too much. She wouldn't have been the only pregnant woman to go to class.

"Merrick was pretty pissed when she got pregnant. He gave her such a hard time. I don't think he ever gave a damn about Ella. I don't know why he even married her. Things went to shit quick, and they didn't get any better as time went on."

Melanie's contempt was obvious. She took a swig of her beer, shaking her head in disgust. "He's just out whoring around."

Hearing the tale of Ella's betrayal, my body tensed. Memories of Tim flooded me with humiliation, twisting the knife again. I wasn't even married to Tim, and I had been devastated. I can't imagine what Ella must have gone through.

"Has she had the baby yet?" I asked.

"I'm sure she has." Melanie frowned in thought. "Should have been a month or two ago. I can't remember."

My jaw dropped. "That's ridiculous. Maybe if he wasn't out getting his *dick* wet, his wife would have stayed at home."

"I can't imagine." Melanie took another swig of beer. "She's gone and rumor is that he's been out running around flashing cash with some other woman. Lynn, Leah…It doesn't matter. The guy's a prick."

I picked up my shot glass and raised it toward the waitress in time to see him slide his keys and credit card across the bar. With the glow of the reflection, I could see he was disheveled but still wickedly handsome. His dark hair was tousled and a days' growth of stubble peppered his face. He reminded me of the men in my own family, and a twinge of anger shot through me.

The Steele men had a reputation. Hell, I was the only girl, and *I* had a reputation. Before Tim, I was known to give a guy a run for his money, but I couldn't imagine my brothers treating their future wives like that. Our dad would go off the deep end. Women were a gift and a wife was a treasure. Disrespect to either…yeah, you didn't want to go there.

"I hope she gets what she deserves," I mumbled. "That's some bullshit right there."

"Yup. He oughta be home taking care of his girl, not out here picking up skanks."

The waitress delivered another round of shots, which we tipped back without the aid of salt or lime. Neither of us believed in accessorizing and ruining good tequila.

"She's not his girl, Melanie." My thinking was fuzzy, but her comment made my ears burn. They were married for Christ sake. With a baby! "She's his wife," I corrected her. "And she ought to take every dime she can get."

Melanie dismissed the idea with a wave of her hand. "She doesn't need the money."

I scoffed at her response. "It's not about what she needs, it's about what she deserves," I explained. "Every dime he's got, even the ones under the cushions for the shit he's done."

My own betrayal gave me the wisdom to speak on such things, and I spoke my opinion with conviction. Melanie grabbed her beer and raised it in agreement. "With some proof, she just might."

She leaned in to me and I instinctively met her in the space that separated our stools. "The *little* brain must have a *massive* dysfunction if a man who looks like *that* has to buy women." Melanie laughed, a sound of drunken hysteria that rose above the music and drew the attention of nearby tables.

The music was fading around me, and I cut my eyes from Merrick Kincaid to Melanie, the alcohol racing through my blood. My common decency battled with the primal attraction that raged inside of me—a pure chemical reaction based on his physical perfection and my poor judgment. The words came out before I could stop them.

"Shit, I'd fuck him for free."

Melanie's eyes shot up in surprise before she burst out laughing. "Sweetheart, he wouldn't give you a second look."

I stiffened and my body washed warm with embarrassment. "What are you saying, Melanie?"

She patted my arm in the way that drunks pacify other drunks. "Calm down, hellcat. I'm just saying you're not exactly Merrick's type. You're complete opposite of Ella, pale and redheaded, short and...well, knowing Ella, I'd bet Mr. Kincaid is an ass man. You, my friend, are all boobs."

Without thinking, I braced my arms on the stool and ejected myself from my perch. The quick movement seemed to send the alcohol that had been pooling in my belly throughout my system, and I upset the table. At that moment the band announced a break and the room went quiet without the echo of the music pounding from the speakers. The empty bottles dancing on the upset table rang out like tolling bells. Melanie grabbed and steadied the bottles as I palmed my boobs and pushed them up.

"Well, you get your phone ready for the pictures, and we'll just see about that."

Trinity has inherited a bit of that feistiness that I became so fond of in Margaret. A little misplaced, no doubt, but just when Trinity seems to be getting her life back together, Merrick finds reason to destroy it all.

Is she strong enough to convince him that love is greater than his pain? If she can't, none of the Steele's may survive the wrath of Merrick.

Mercy Denied

is scheduled for release early 2016.

About the Author

Jacqueline grew up in the rural southeast and is the youngest child of a large and rowdy family. Reading was an escape when there wasn't much else around to do. She loves everything from classical literature to true crime and everything in between. With her two children grown and gone, she's surrounded by a menagerie of adopted pets and a two-legged thief who refused to give her heart back after a night of karaoke.

With a day job and a dream job, her writing is a steamy combination of real life and seeking to answer the age-old question of what would happen if...and then characters evolve and completely derail the plan. Letting them have their say provides plenty of sleepless nights and an endless combination of coffee and wine, but she hopes you enjoy their stories.

Connect with Jacqueline for updates and information.
Like on Facebook:
facebook.com/Jacqueline-M-Sinclair-1517706358491729
Friend on Facebook: facebook.com/jacqueline.m.sinclair
Follow on Twitter: www.twitter.com/Jacq2005
Or, email at jacqsinclair@yahoo.com

www.ingramcontent.com/pod-product-compliance
Lightning Source LLC
Chambersburg PA
CBHW070617130626
46556CB00001B/390